ROWA

MW01580560

AVERY
AND THE FAIRY CIRCLE

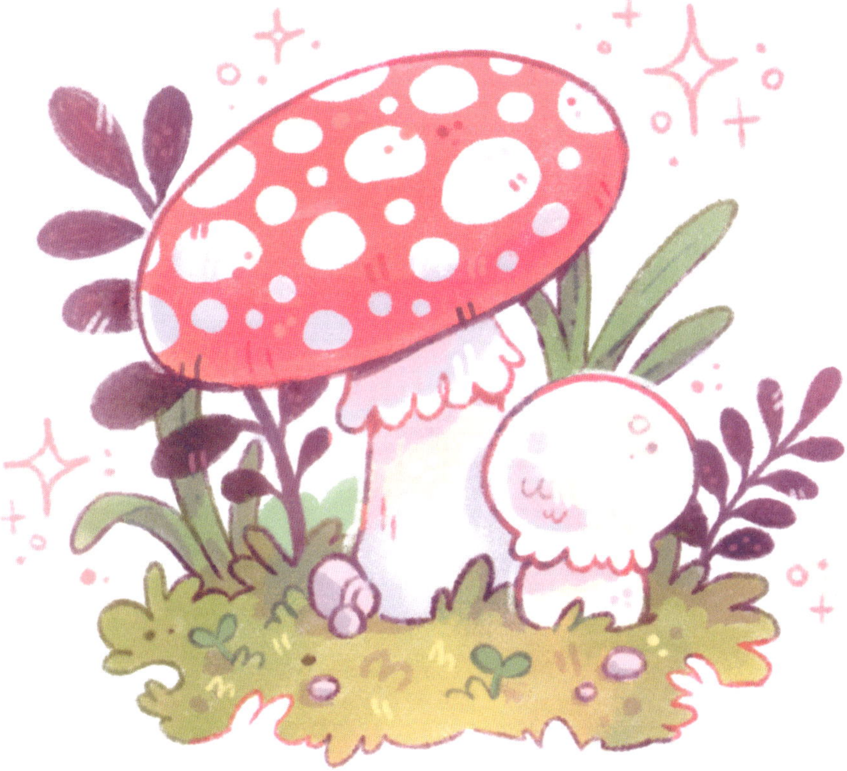

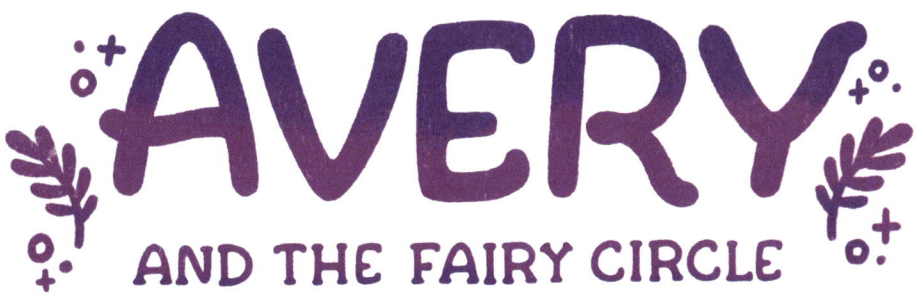

FLYING EYE BOOKS

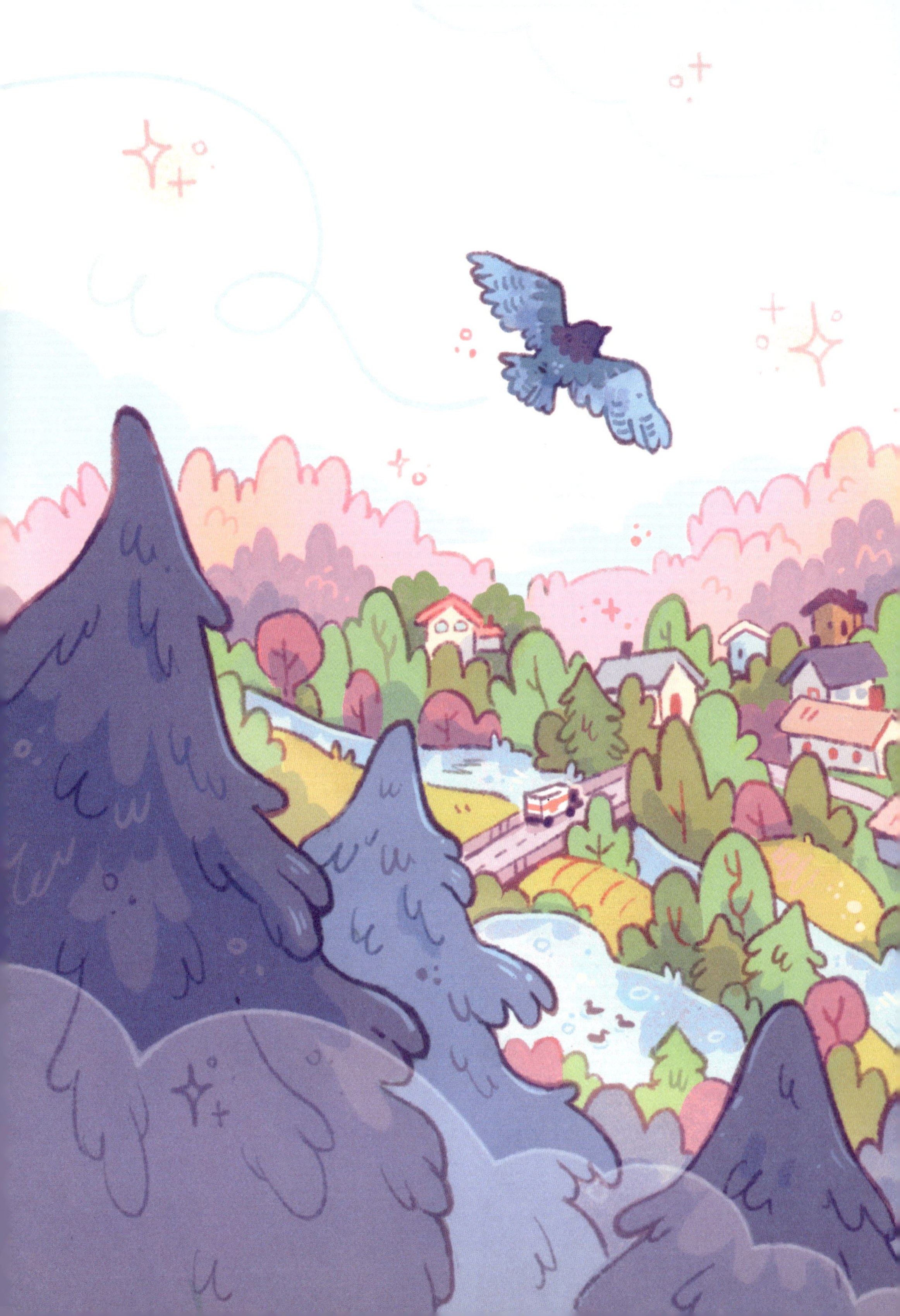

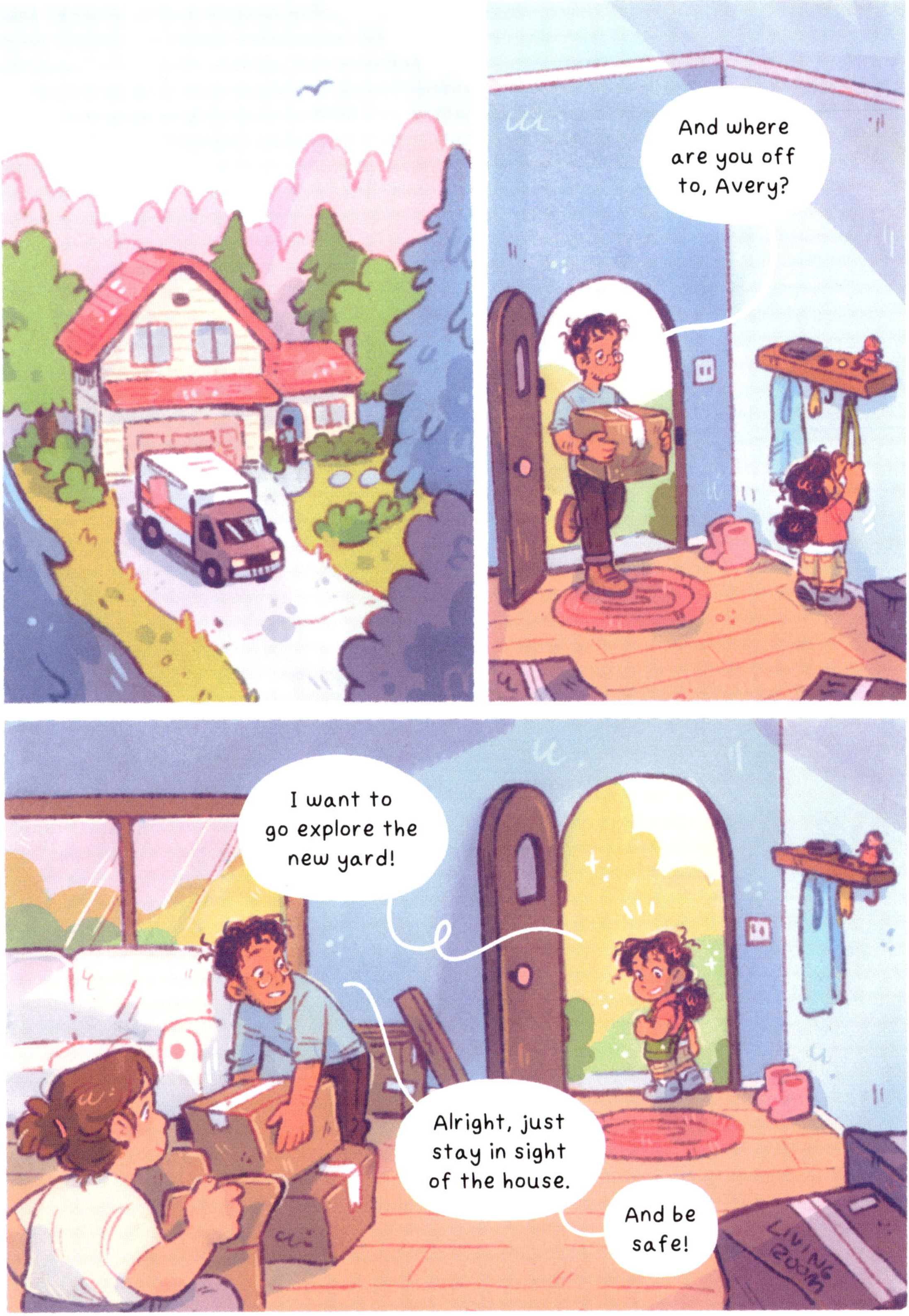
And where are you off to, Avery?
I want to go explore the new yard!
Alright, just stay in sight of the house.
And be safe!
LIVING ROOM

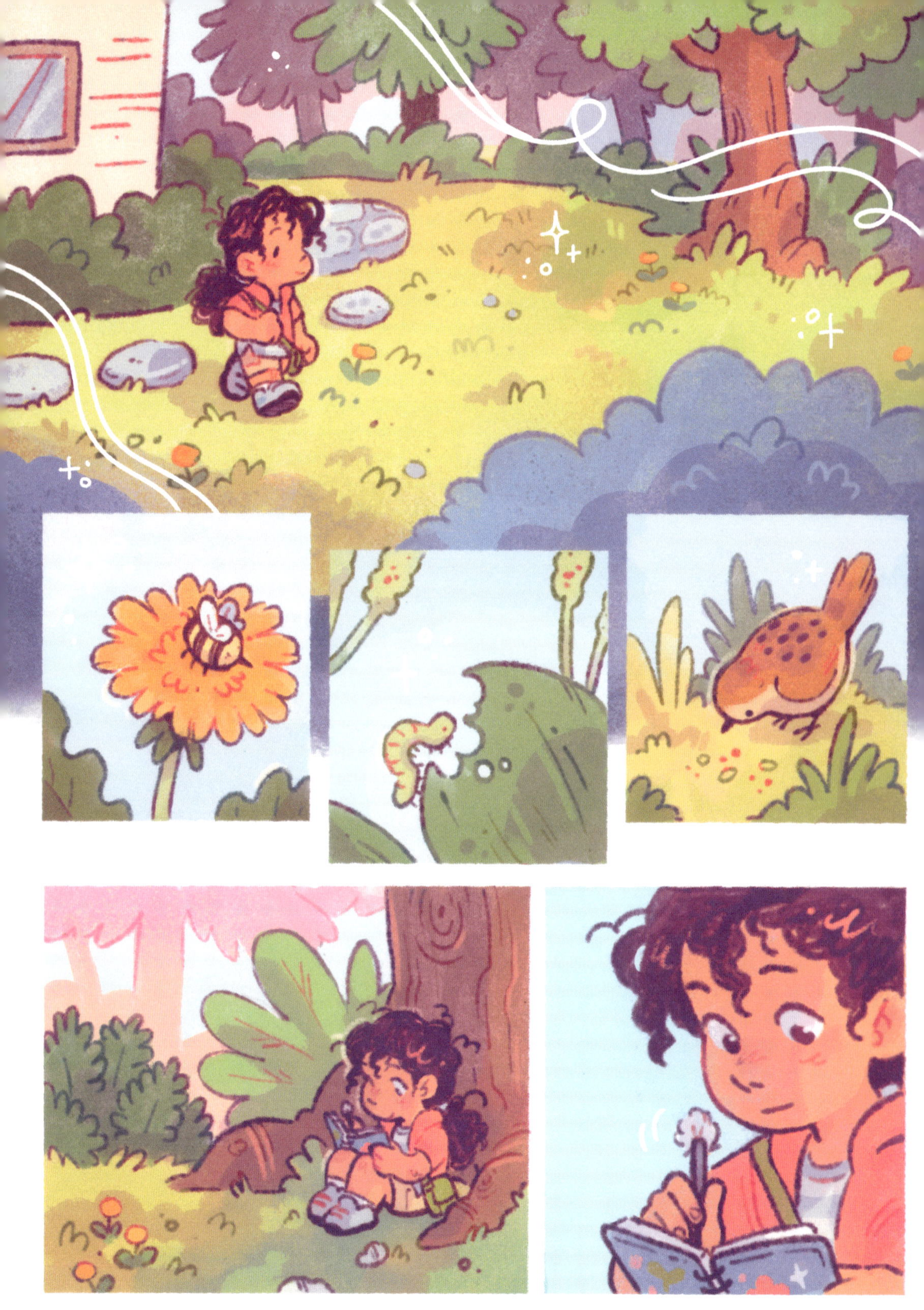

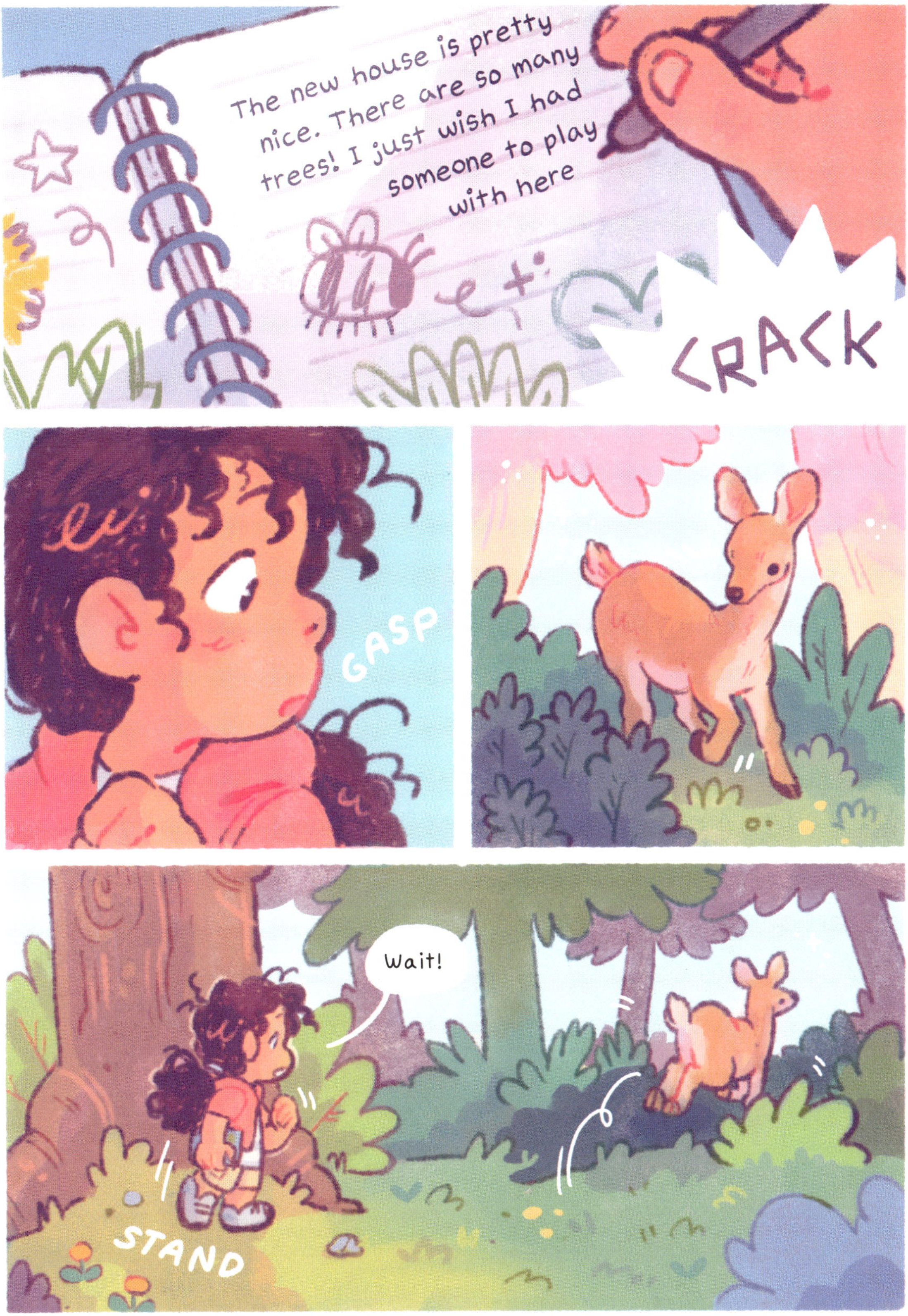
The new house is pretty nice. There are so many trees! I just wish I had someone to play with here
CRACK
GASP
Wait!
STAND

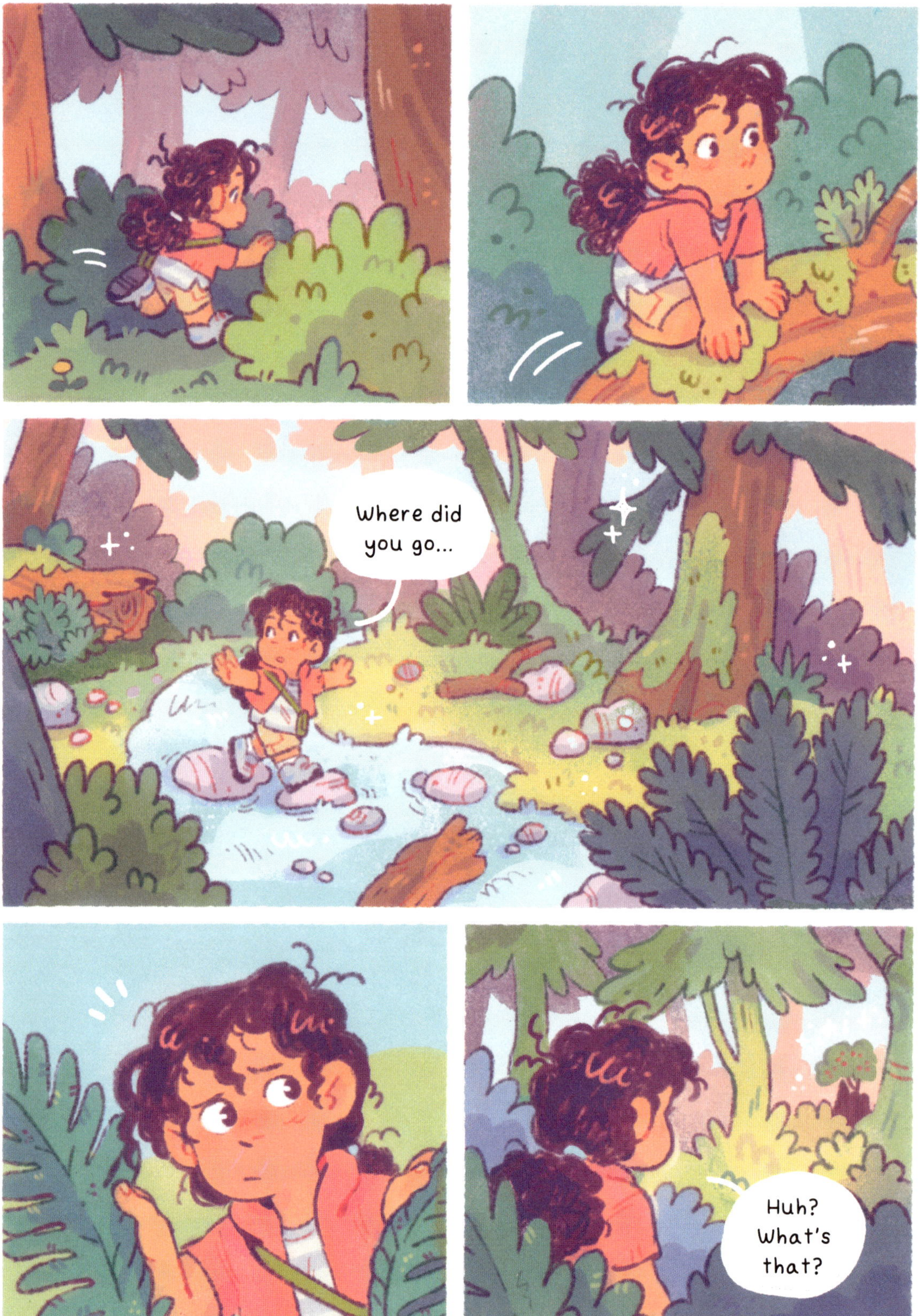
Where did you go...
Huh? What's that?

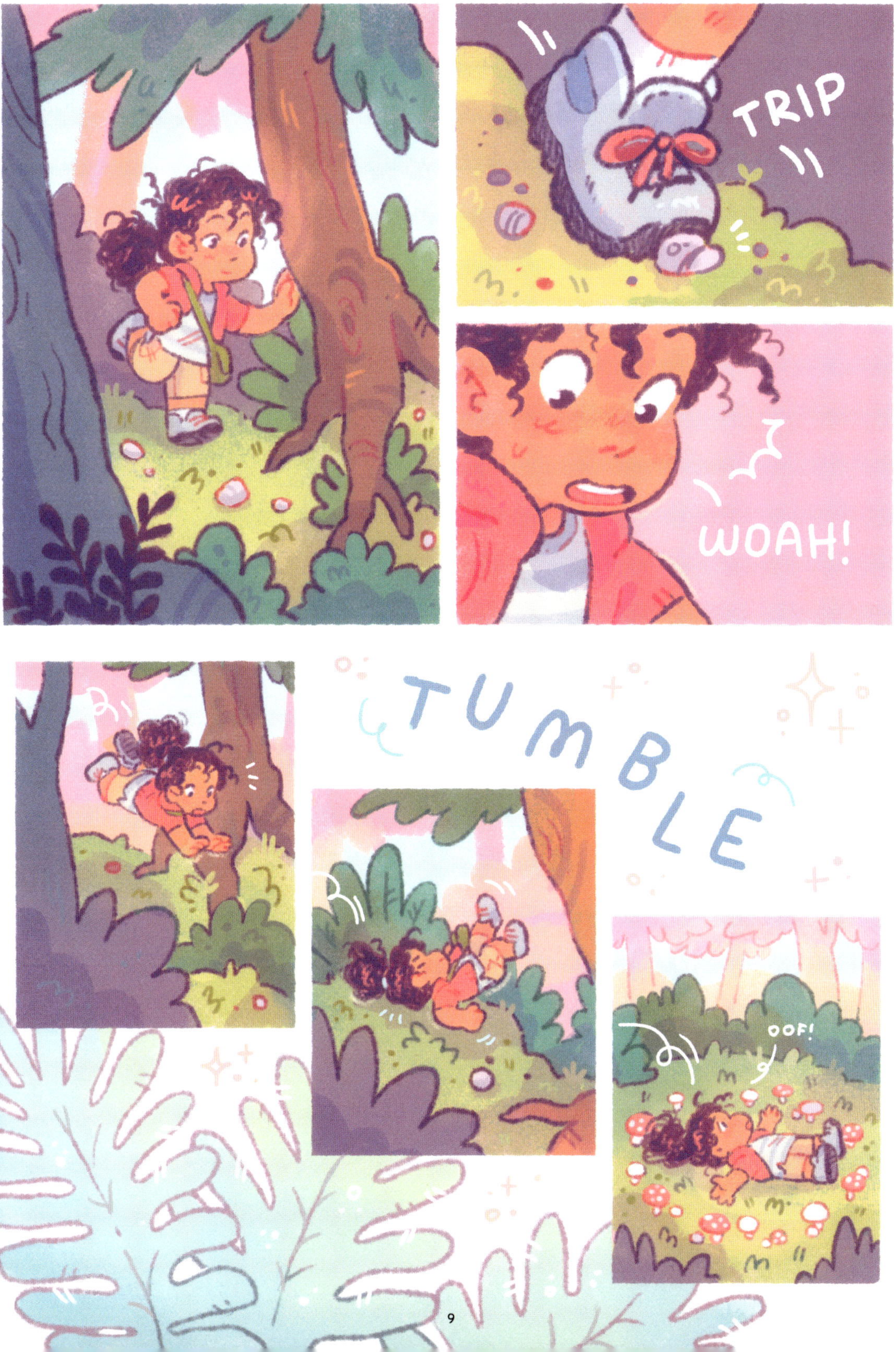
TRIP
WOAH!
TUMBLE
OOF!

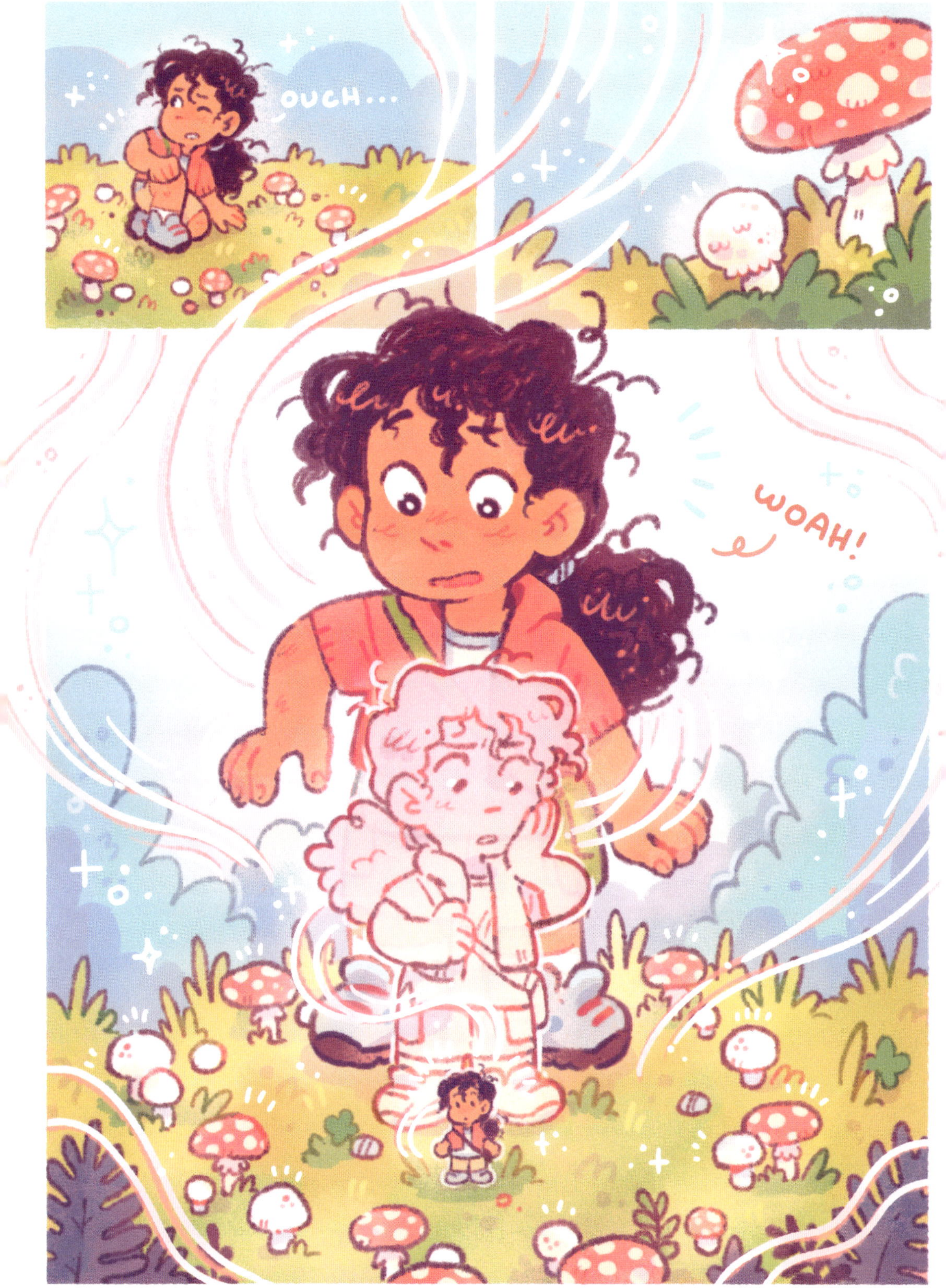
OUCH...
WOAH!

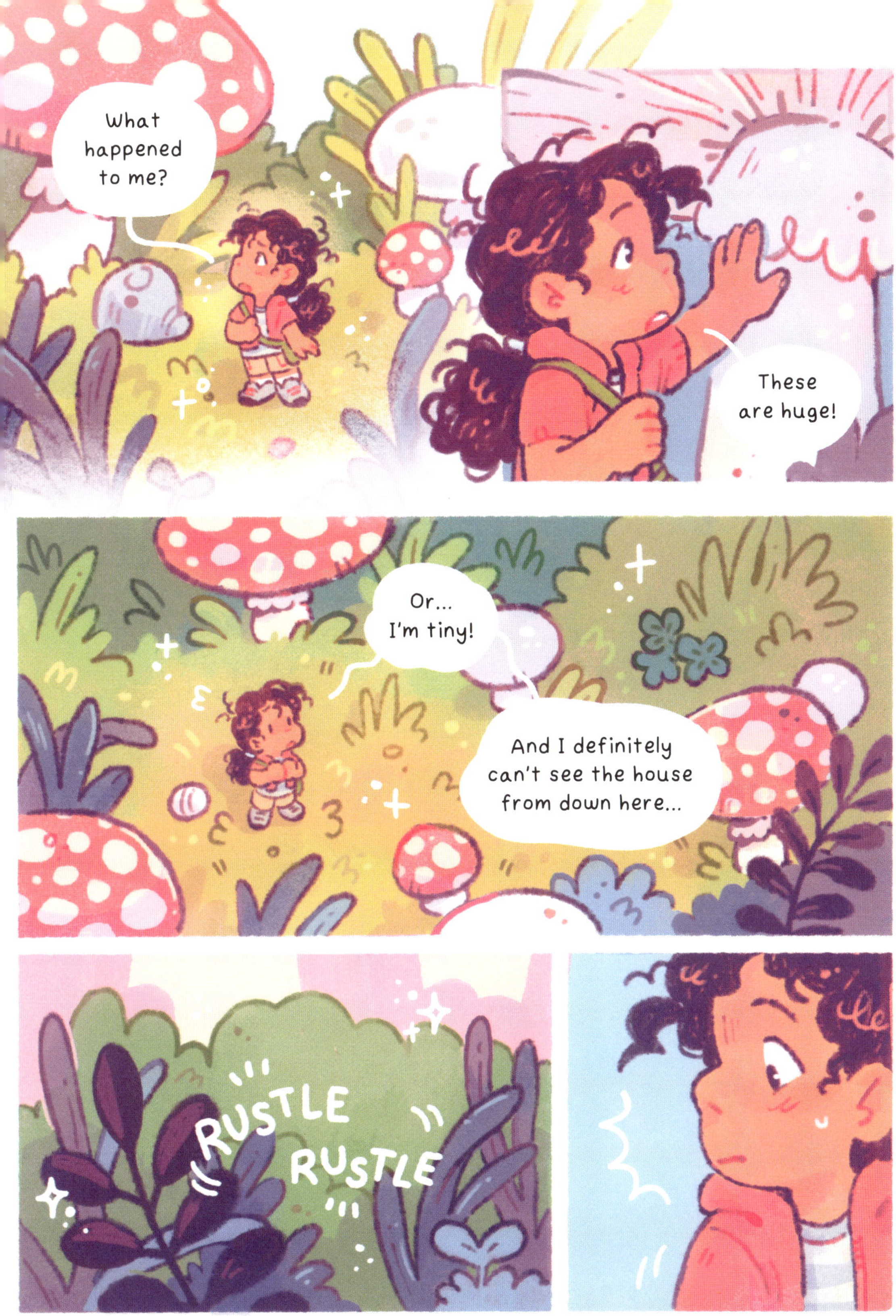
What happened to me?
These are huge!
Or... I'm tiny!
And I definitely can't see the house from down here...
RUSTLE RUSTLE

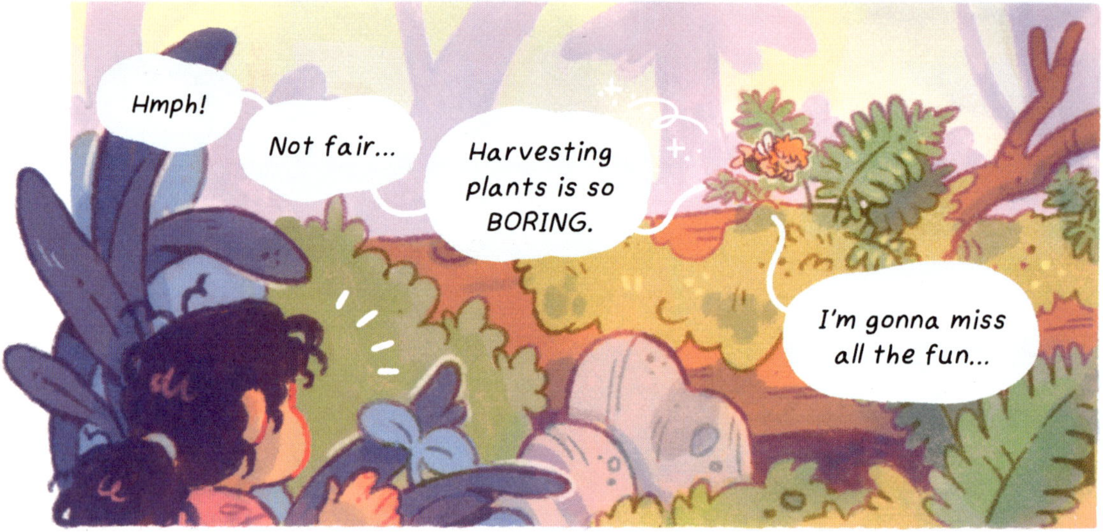
Hmph!
Not fair...
Harvesting plants is so BORING.
I'm gonna miss all the fun...

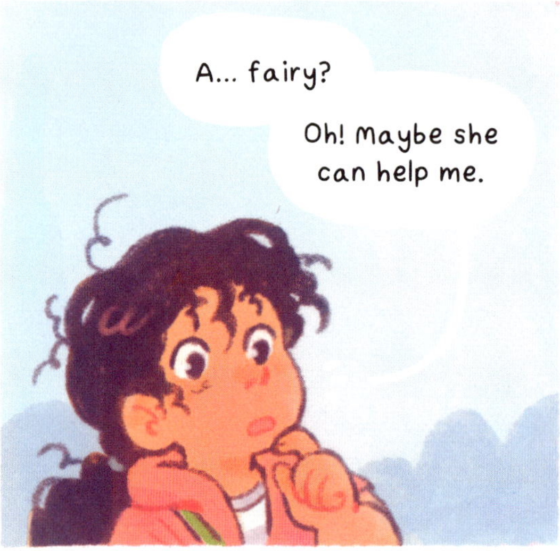
A... fairy?
Oh! Maybe she can help me.

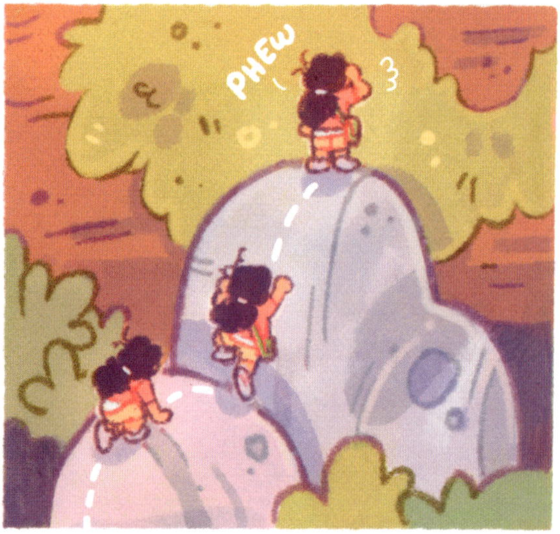
PHEW

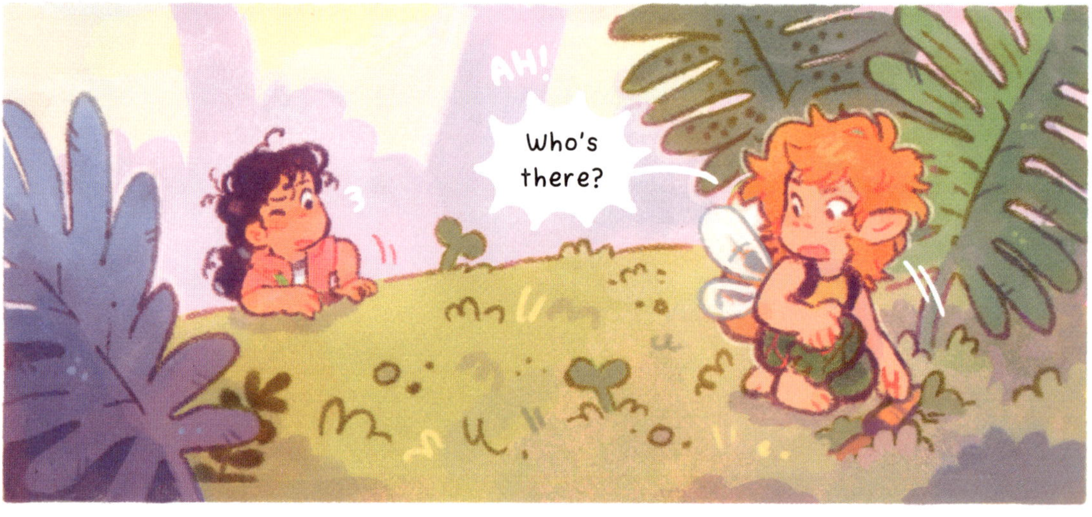
AH!
Who's there?

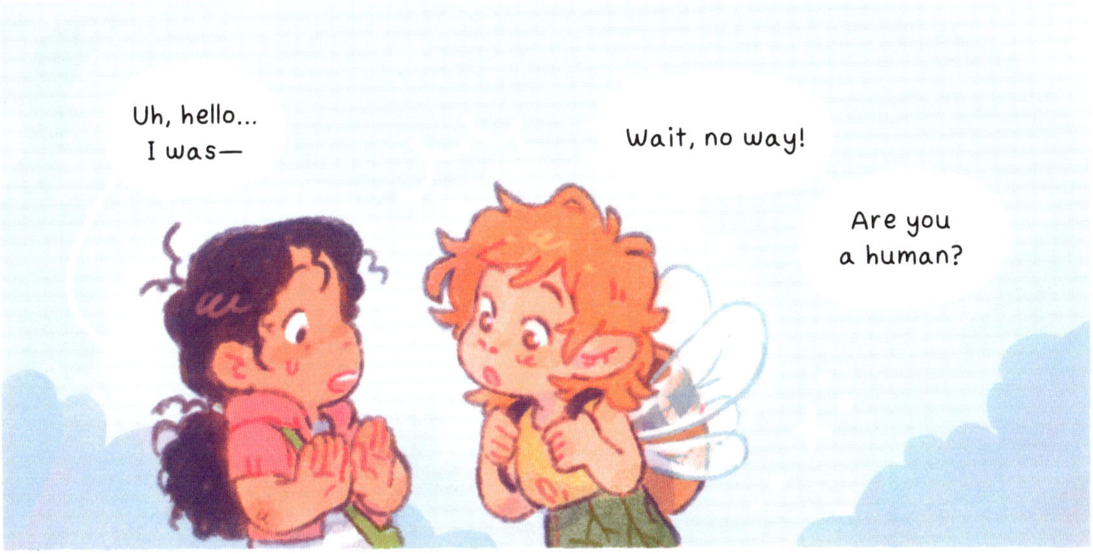
Uh, hello... I was—
Wait, no way!
Are you a human?

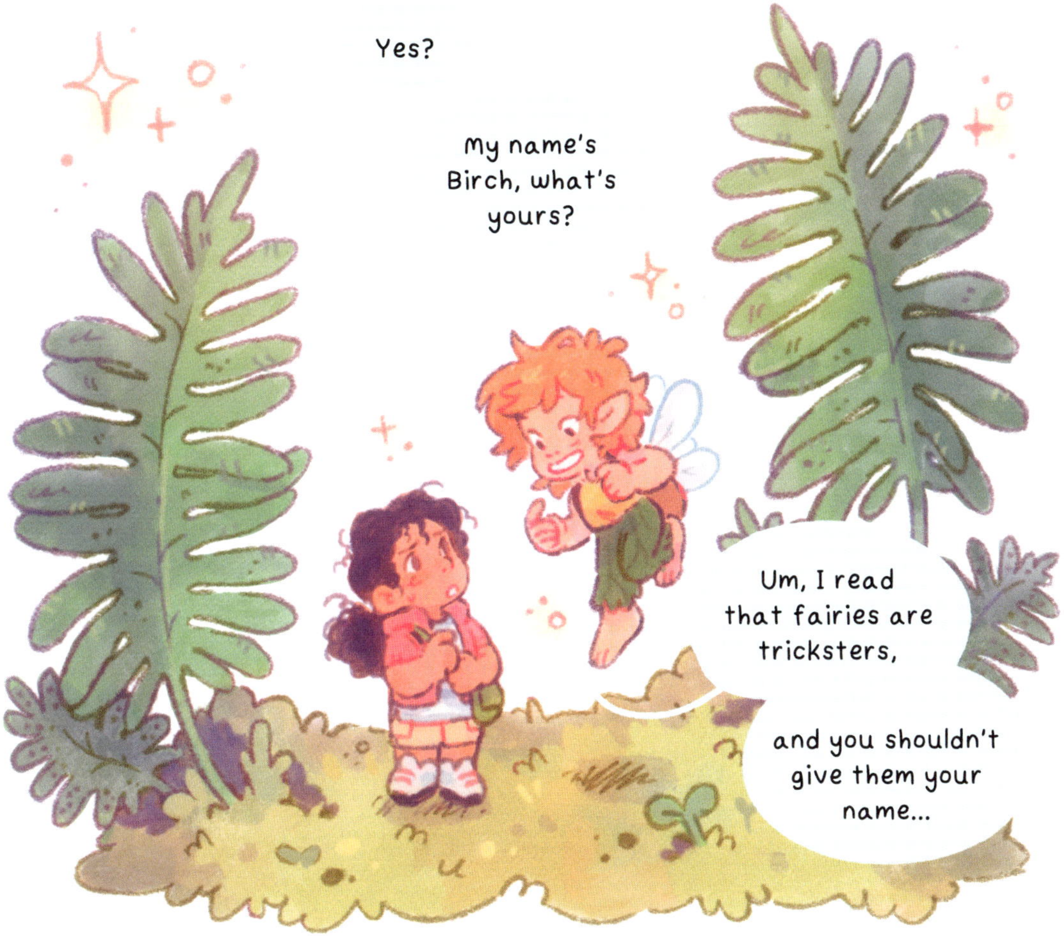
Yes?
My name's Birch, what's yours?
Um, I read that fairies are tricksters,
and you shouldn't give them your name...

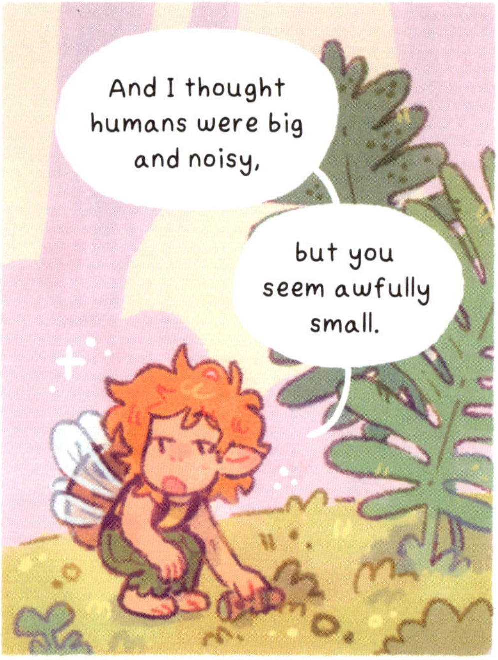
And I thought humans were big and noisy,
but you seem awfully small.

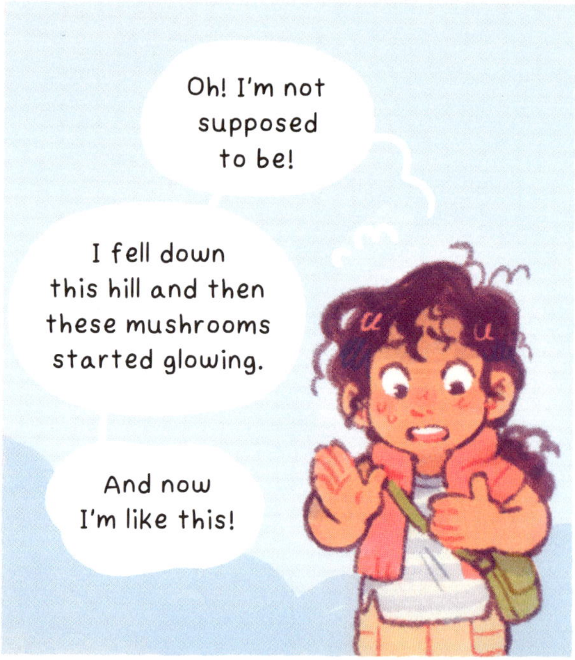
Oh! I'm not supposed to be!
I fell down this hill and then these mushrooms started glowing.
And now I'm like this!

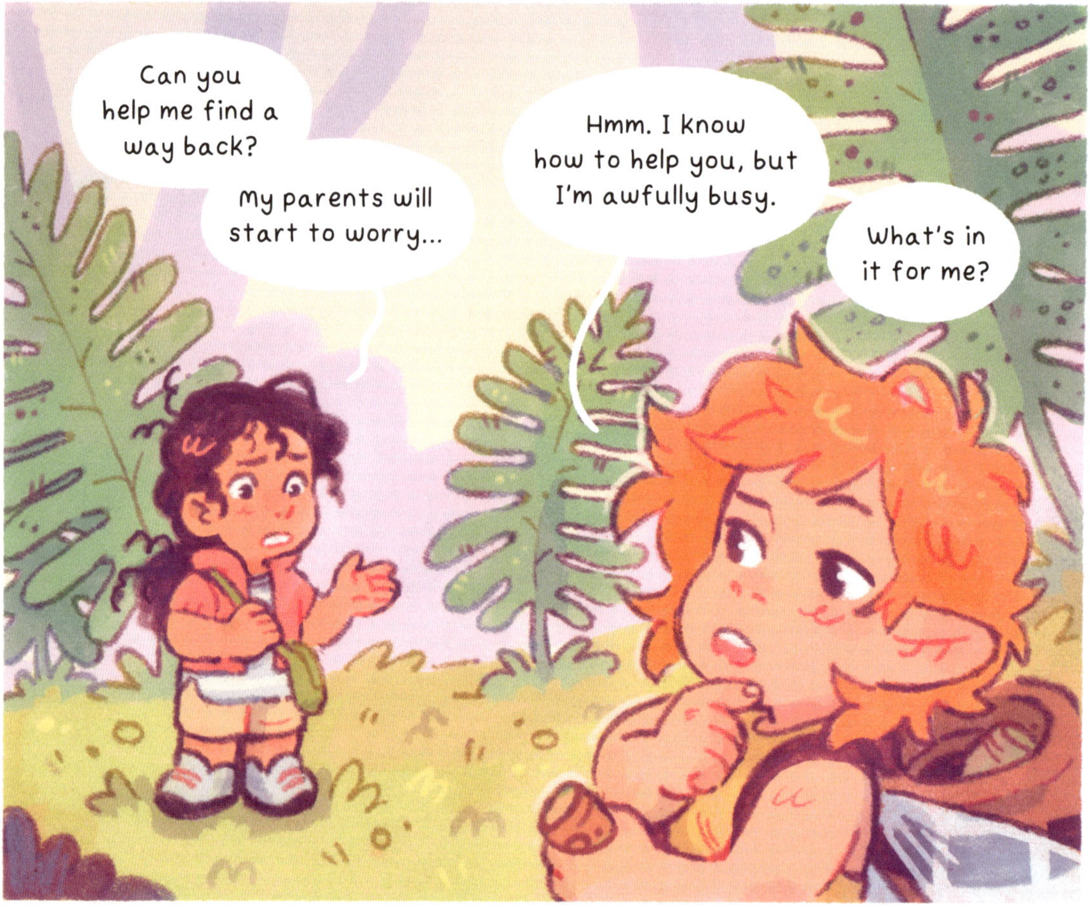
Can you help me find a way back?
My parents will start to worry...
Hmm. I know how to help you, but I'm awfully busy.
What's in it for me?

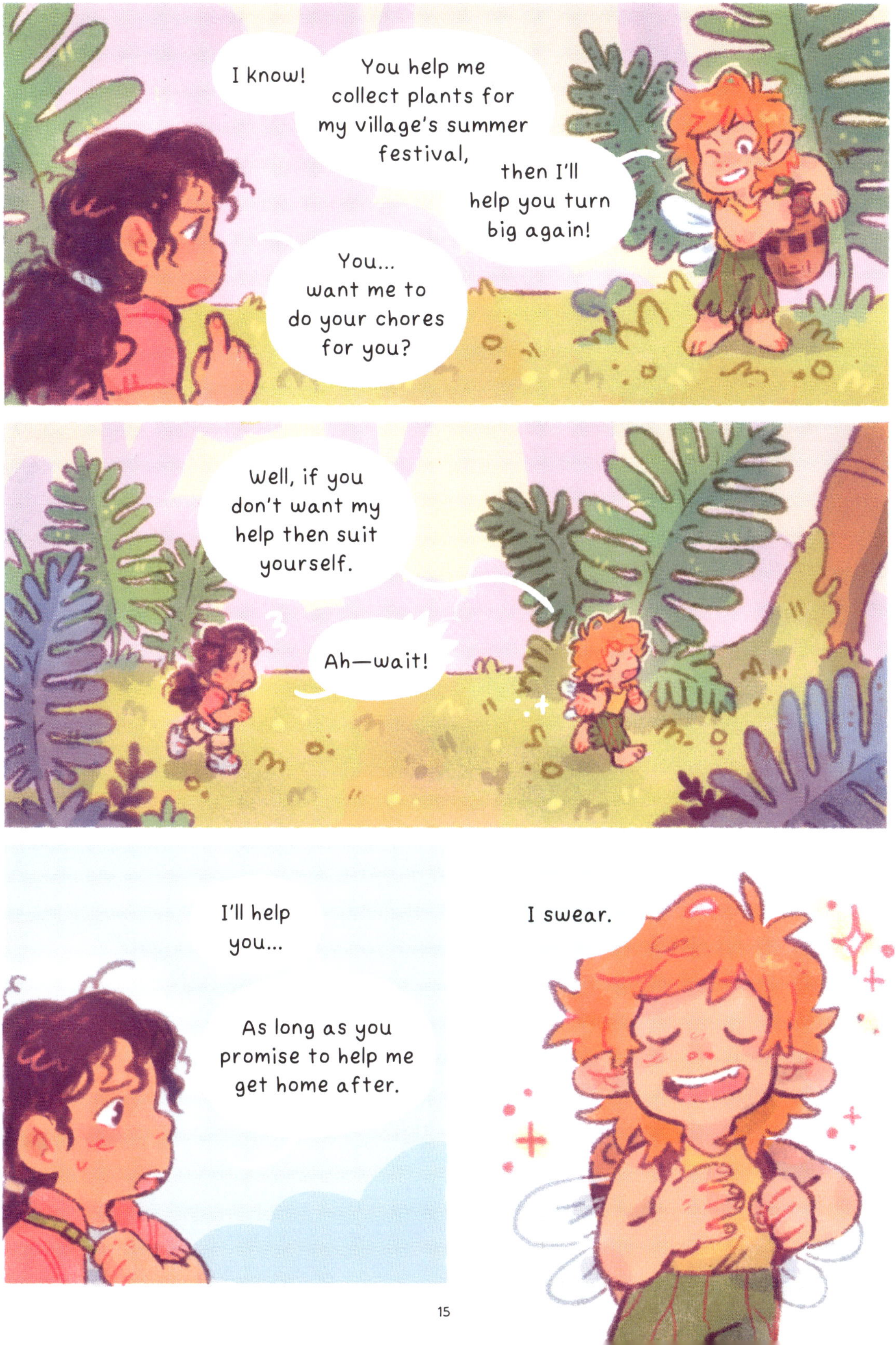
I know!
You help me collect plants for my village's summer festival,
then I'll help you turn big again!
You... want me to do your chores for you?
Well, if you don't want my help then suit yourself.
Ah—wait!
I'll help you...
As long as you promise to help me get home after.
I swear.

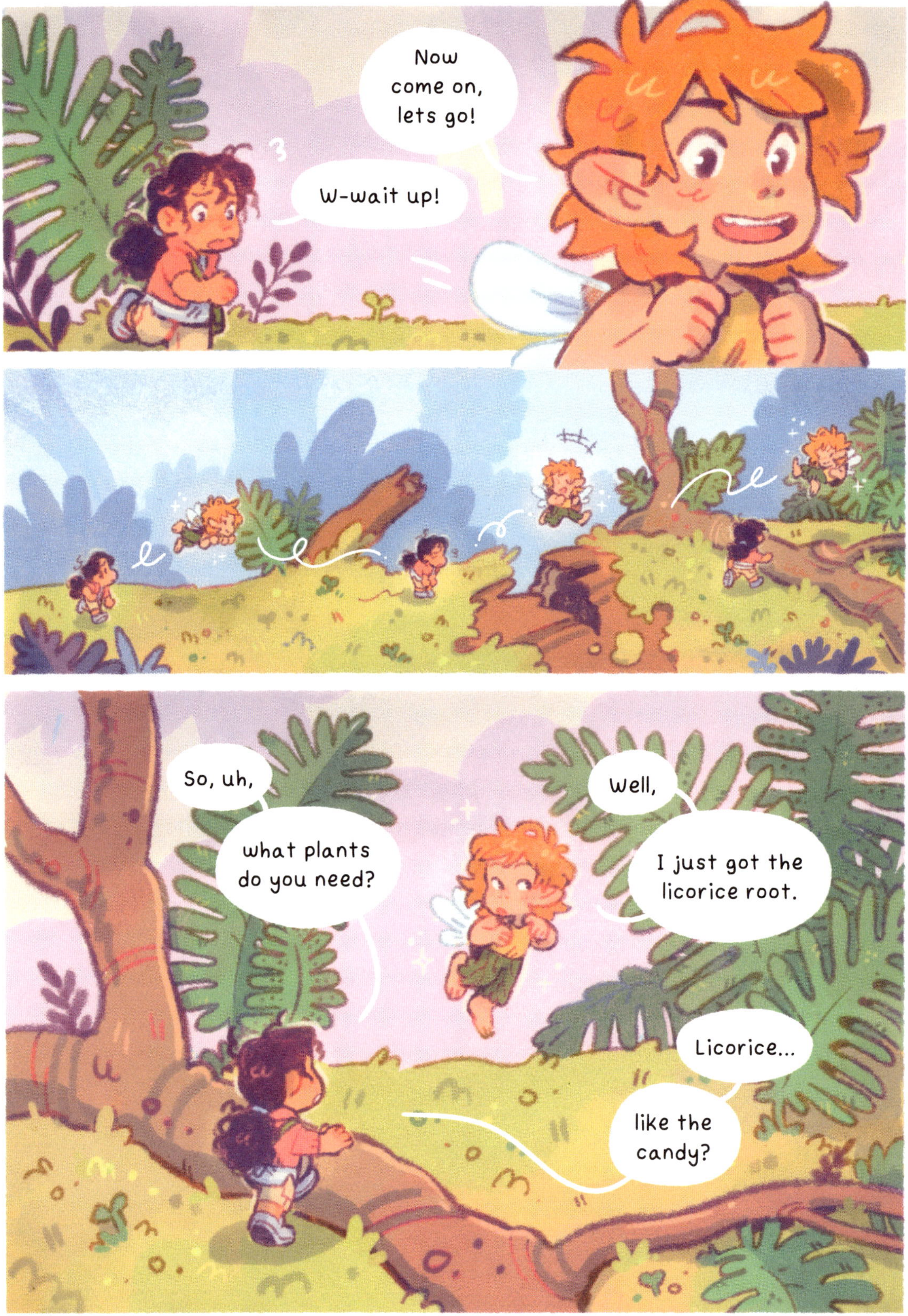
Now come on, lets go!
W-wait up!
So, uh,
what plants do you need?
Well,
I just got the licorice root.
Licorice...
like the candy?

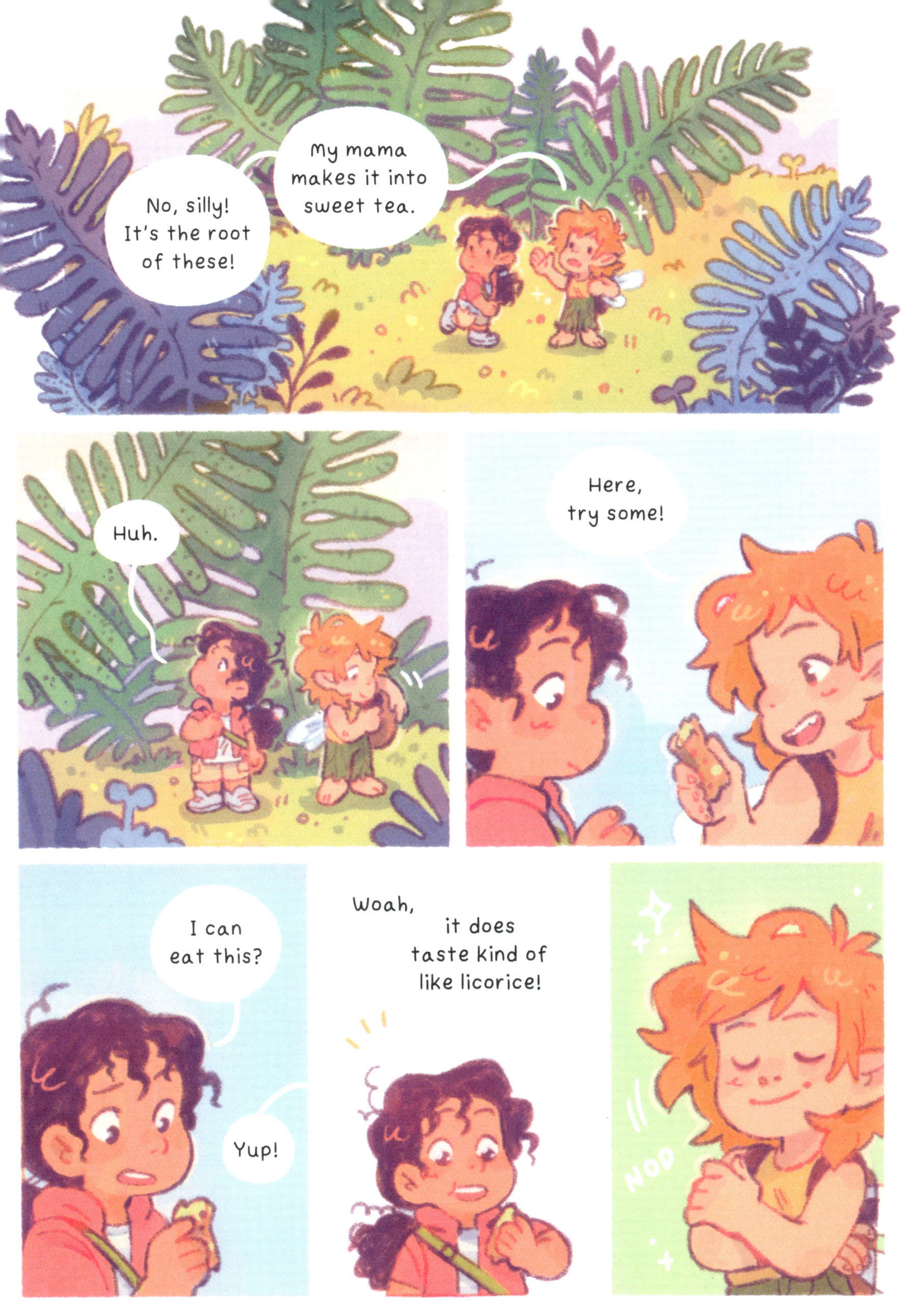
No, silly! It's the root of these!
My mama makes it into sweet tea.
Huh.
Here, try some!
I can eat this?
Yup!
Woah, it does taste kind of like licorice!
NOD

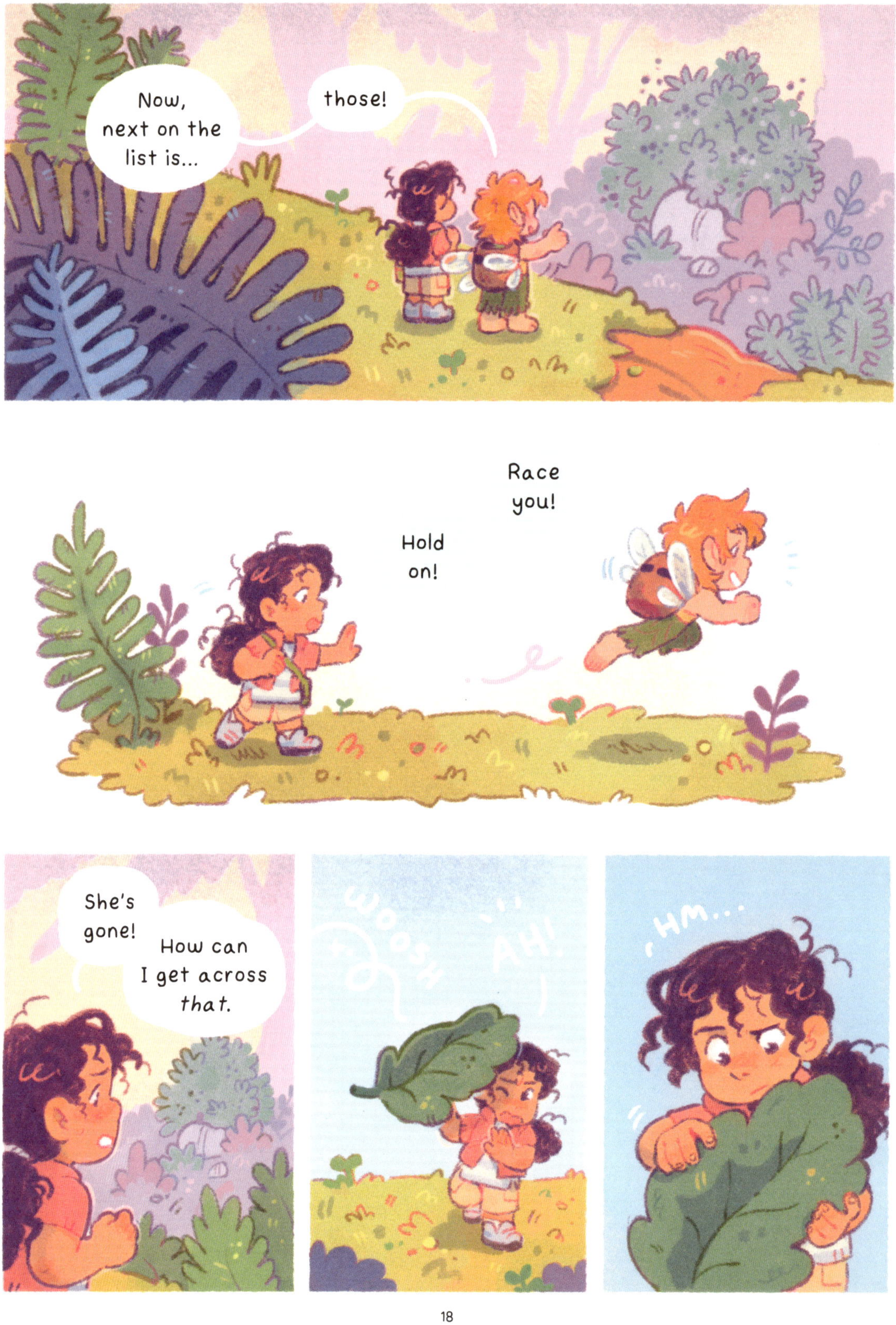
Now, next on the list is...
those!
Race you!
Hold on!
She's gone!
How can I get across *that*.
WOOSH
AH!
HM...

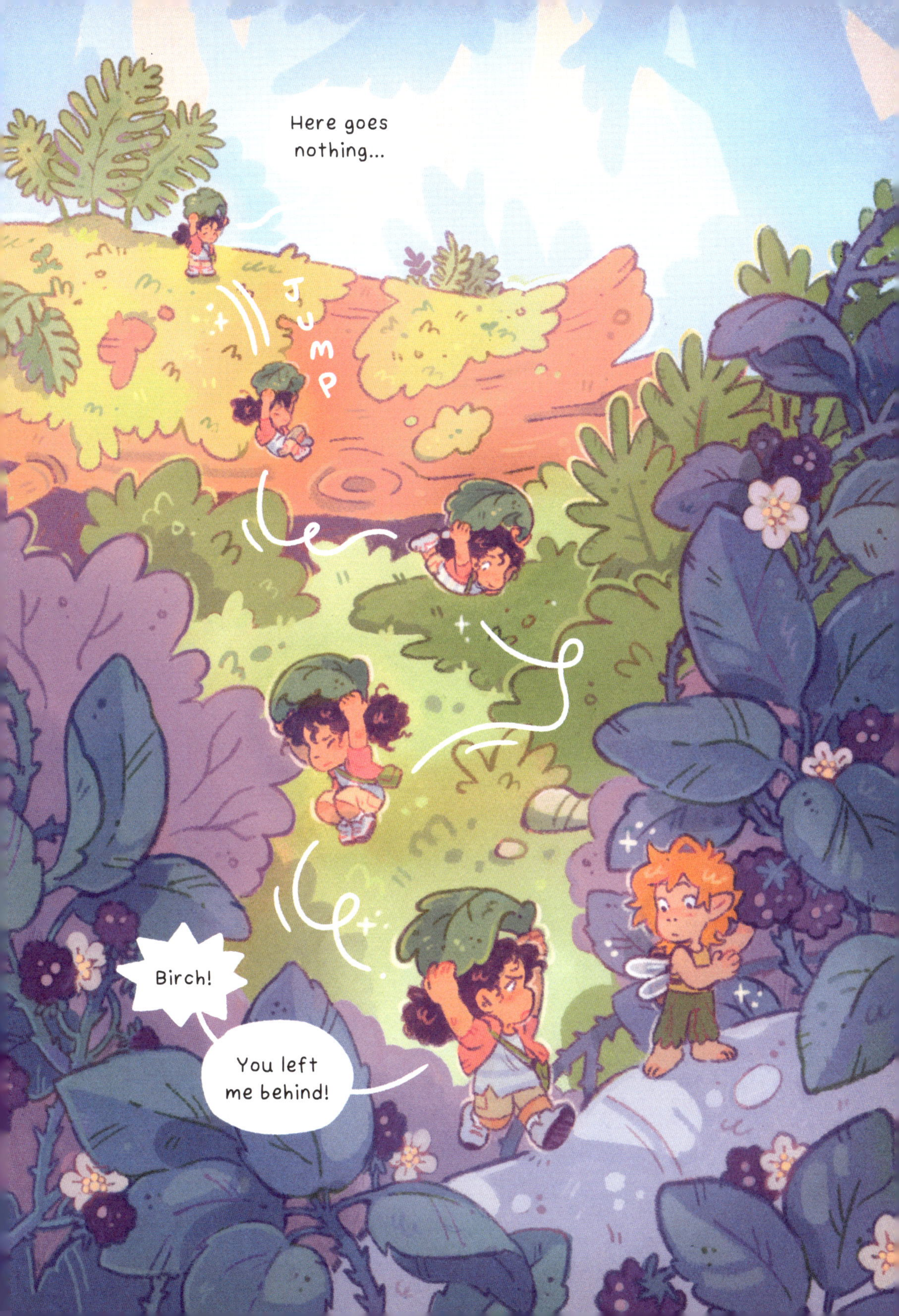
Here goes nothing...
JUMP
Birch!
You left me behind!

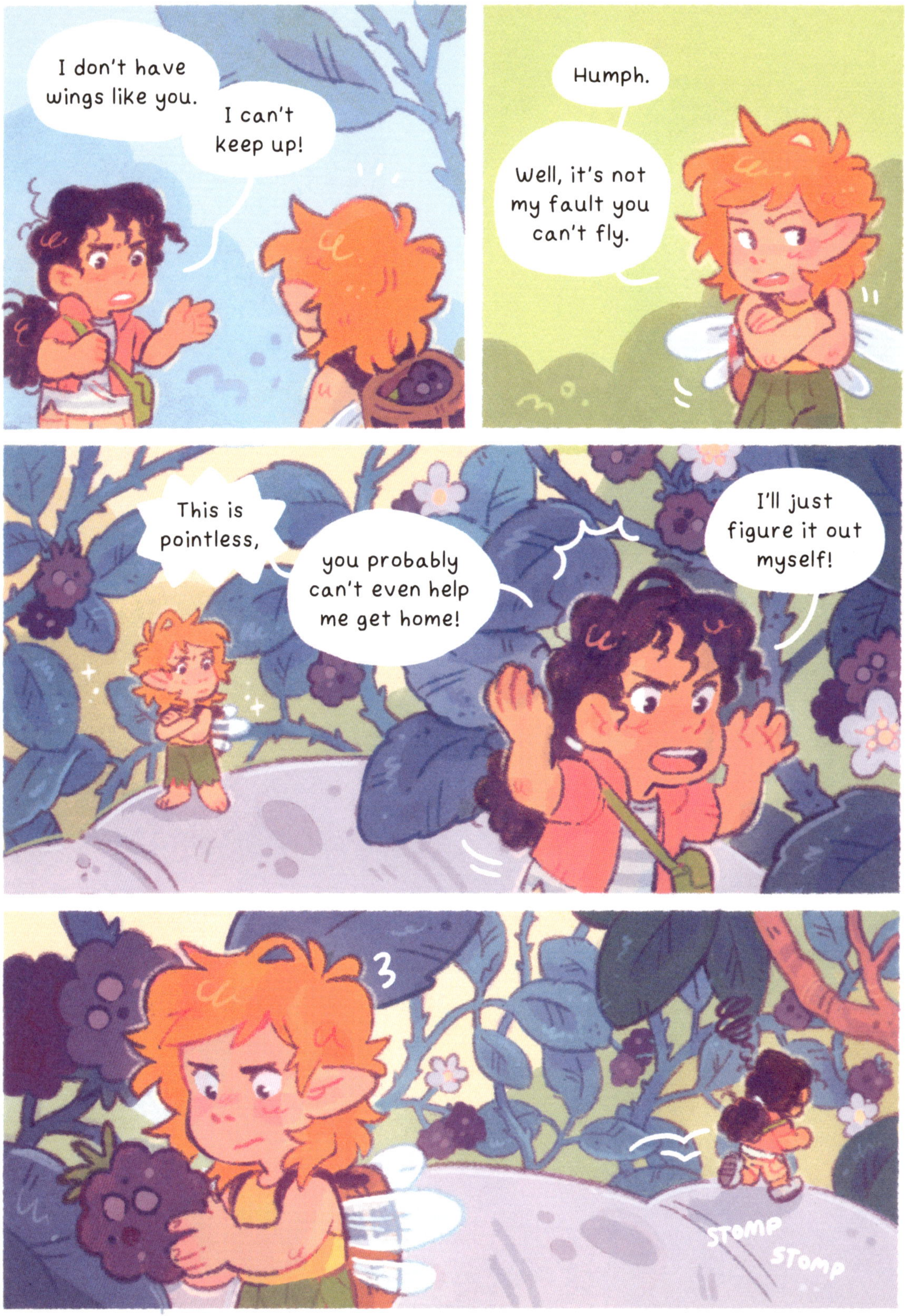
I don't have wings like you.
I can't keep up!
Humph.
Well, it's not my fault you can't fly.
This is pointless,
you probably can't even help me get home!
I'll just figure it out myself!
STOMP
STOMP

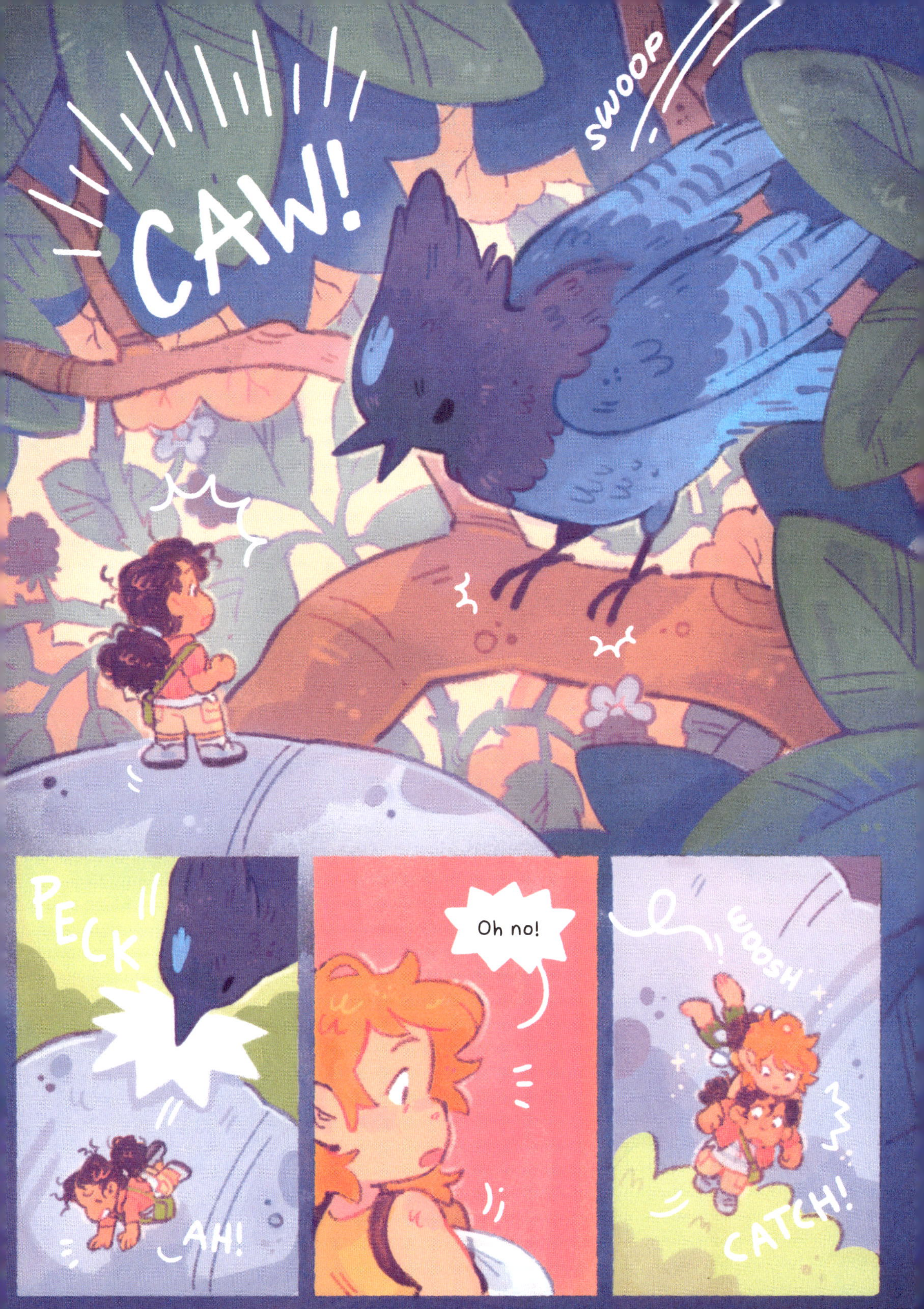
CAW!
SWOOP
PECK
AH!
Oh no!
WOOSH
CATCH!

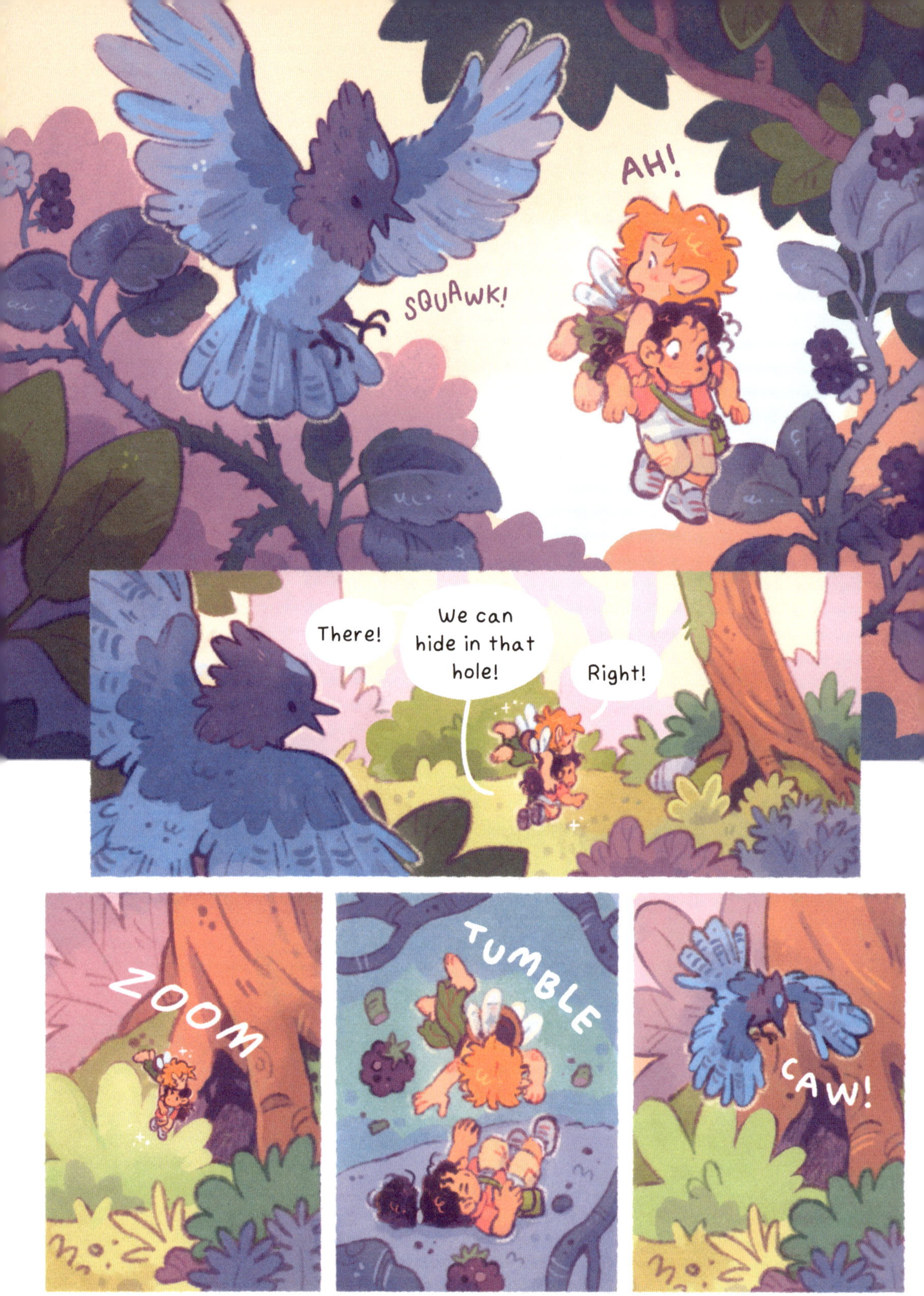
AH!
SQUAWK!
There!
We can hide in that hole!
Right!
ZOOM
TUMBLE
CAW!

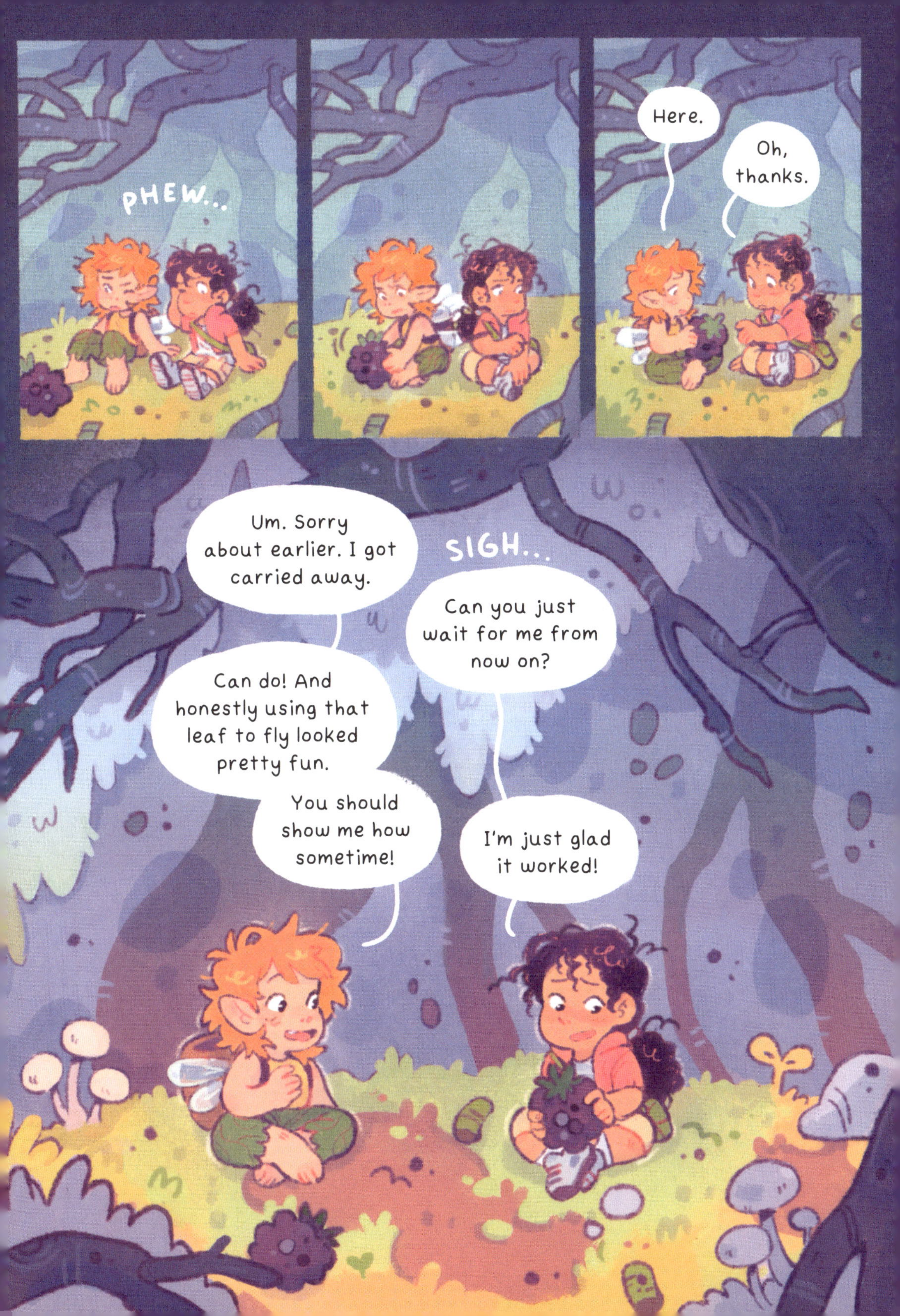
PHEW...
Here.
Oh, thanks.
Um. Sorry about earlier. I got carried away.
SIGH...
Can you just wait for me from now on?
Can do! And honestly using that leaf to fly looked pretty fun.
You should show me how sometime!
I'm just glad it worked!

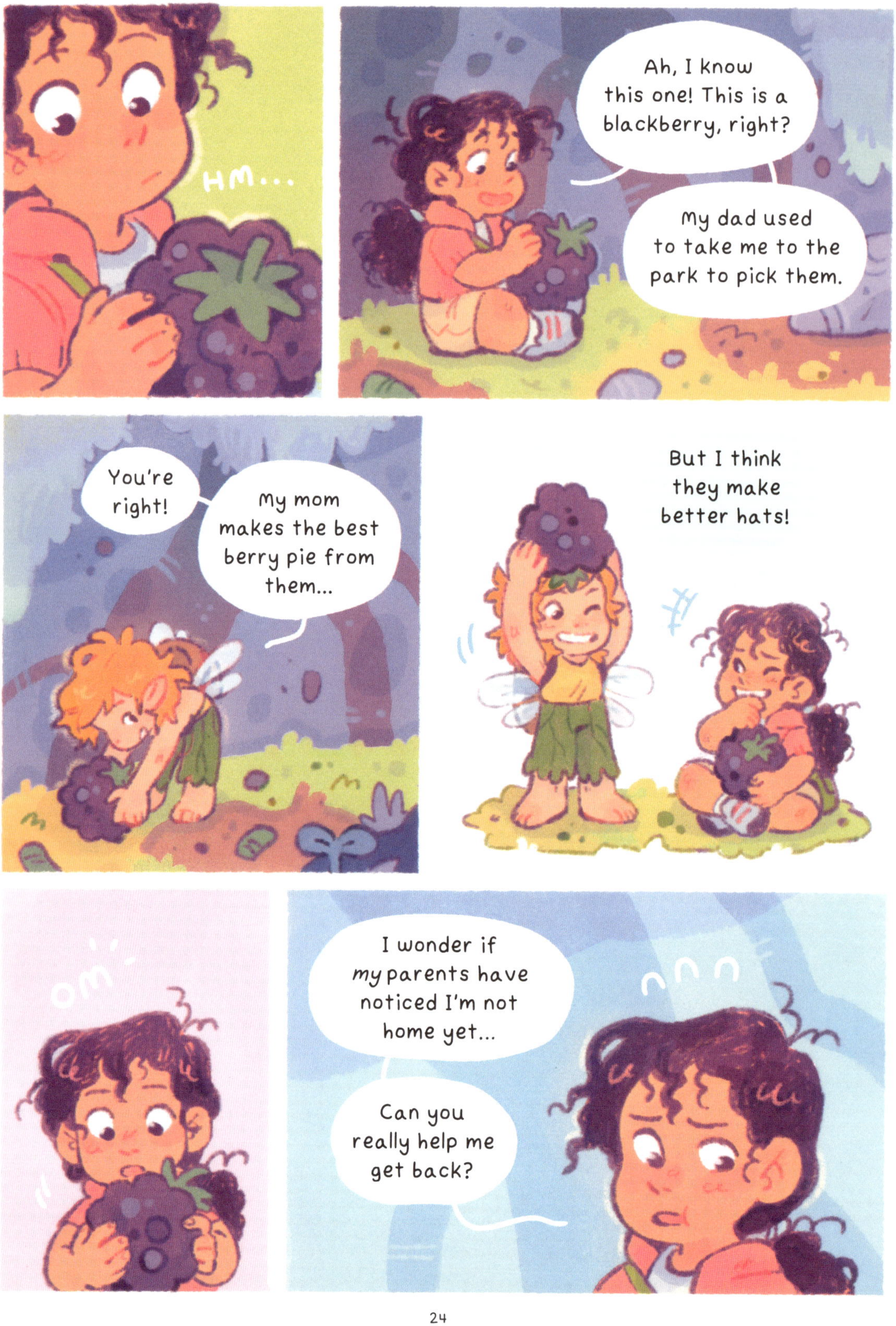
HM...
Ah, I know this one! This is a blackberry, right?
My dad used to take me to the park to pick them.
You're right!
My mom makes the best berry pie from them...
But I think they make better hats!
I wonder if *my* parents have noticed I'm not home yet...
Can you really help me get back?

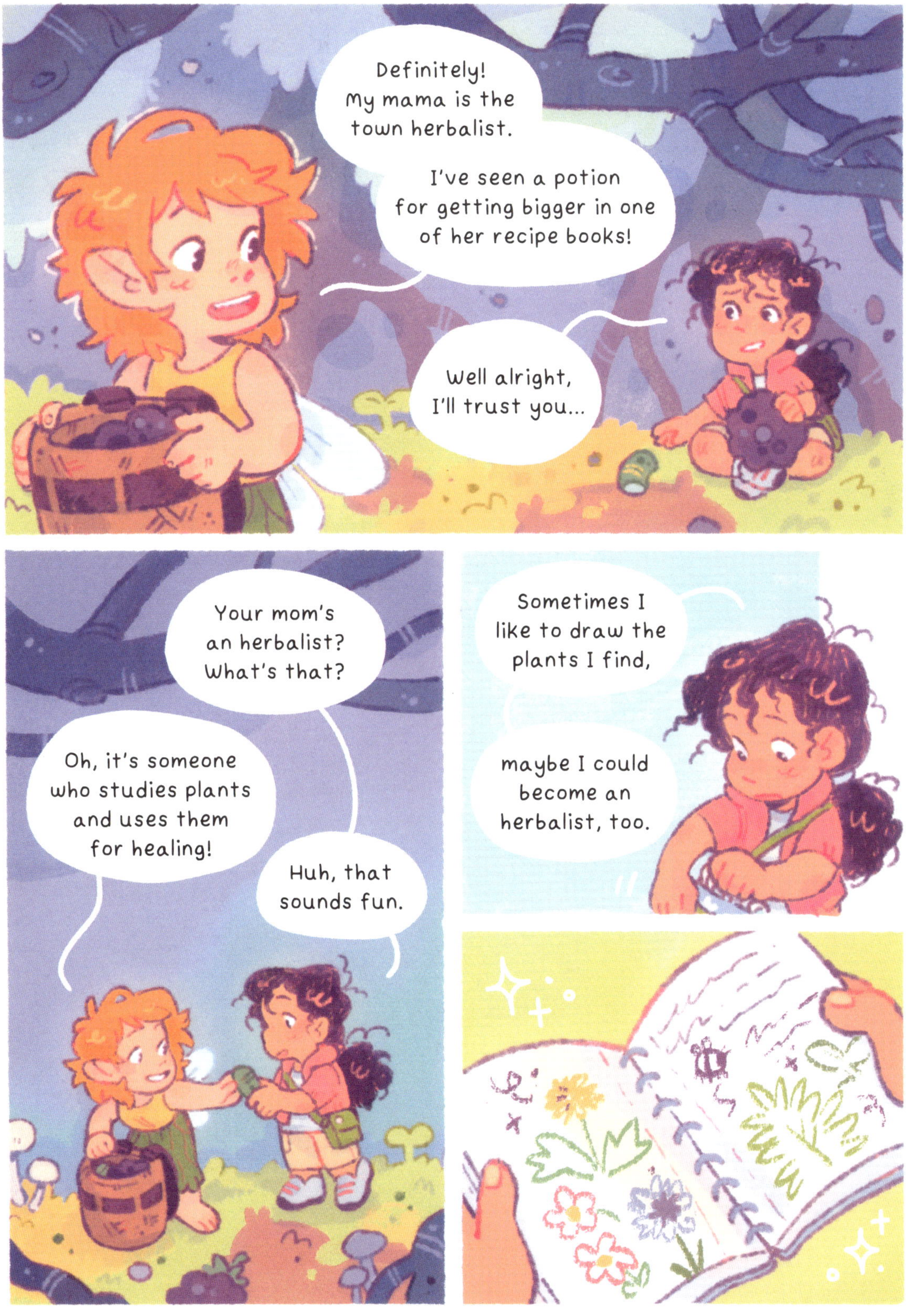
Definitely! My mama is the town herbalist.
I've seen a potion for getting bigger in one of her recipe books!
Well alright, I'll trust you...
Your mom's an herbalist? What's that?
Oh, it's someone who studies plants and uses them for healing!
Huh, that sounds fun.
Sometimes I like to draw the plants I find,
maybe I could become an herbalist, too.

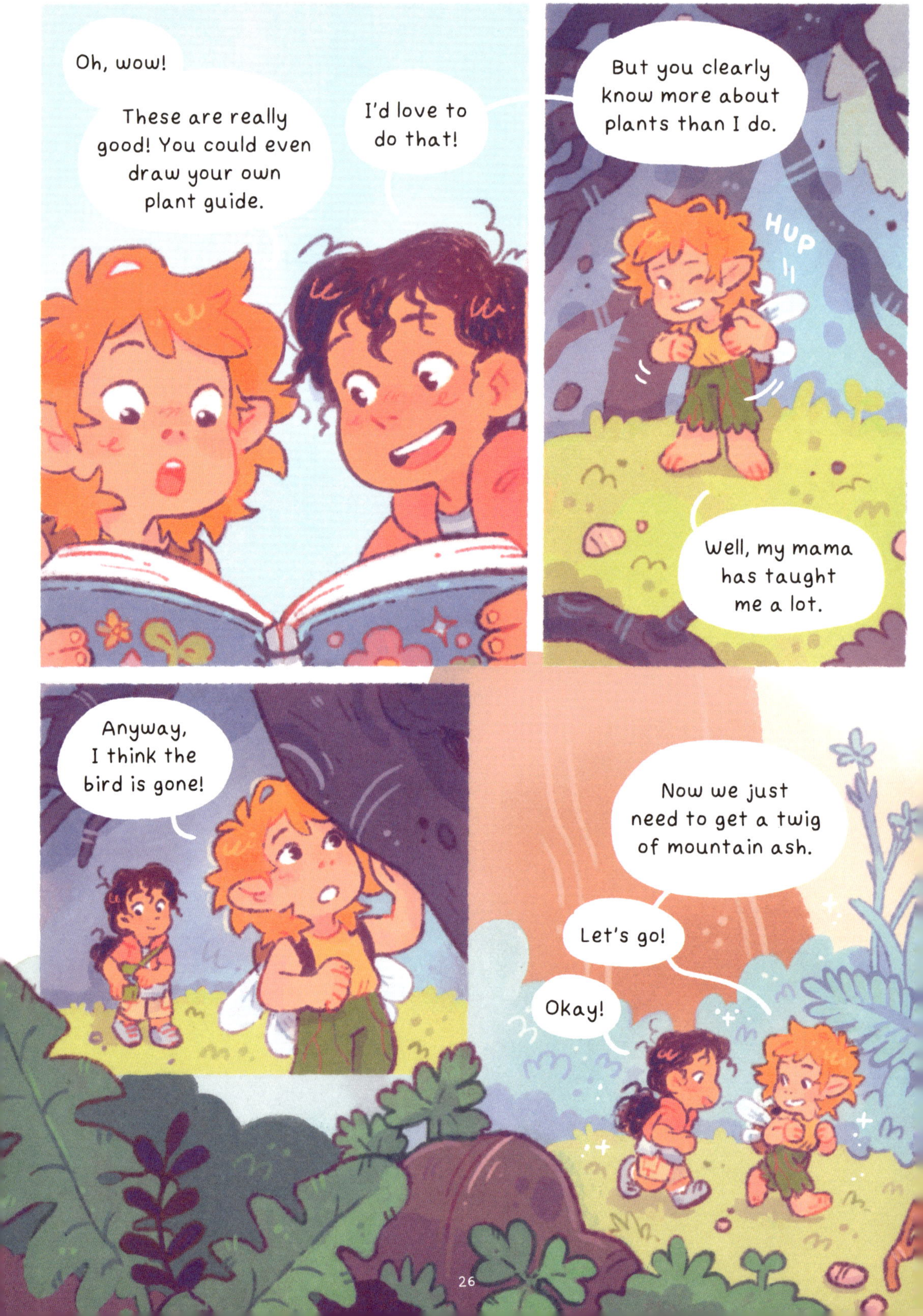
Oh, wow!
These are really good! You could even draw your own plant guide.
I'd love to do that!
But you clearly know more about plants than I do.
HUP
Well, my mama has taught me a lot.
Anyway, I think the bird is gone!
Now we just need to get a twig of mountain ash.
Let's go!
Okay!

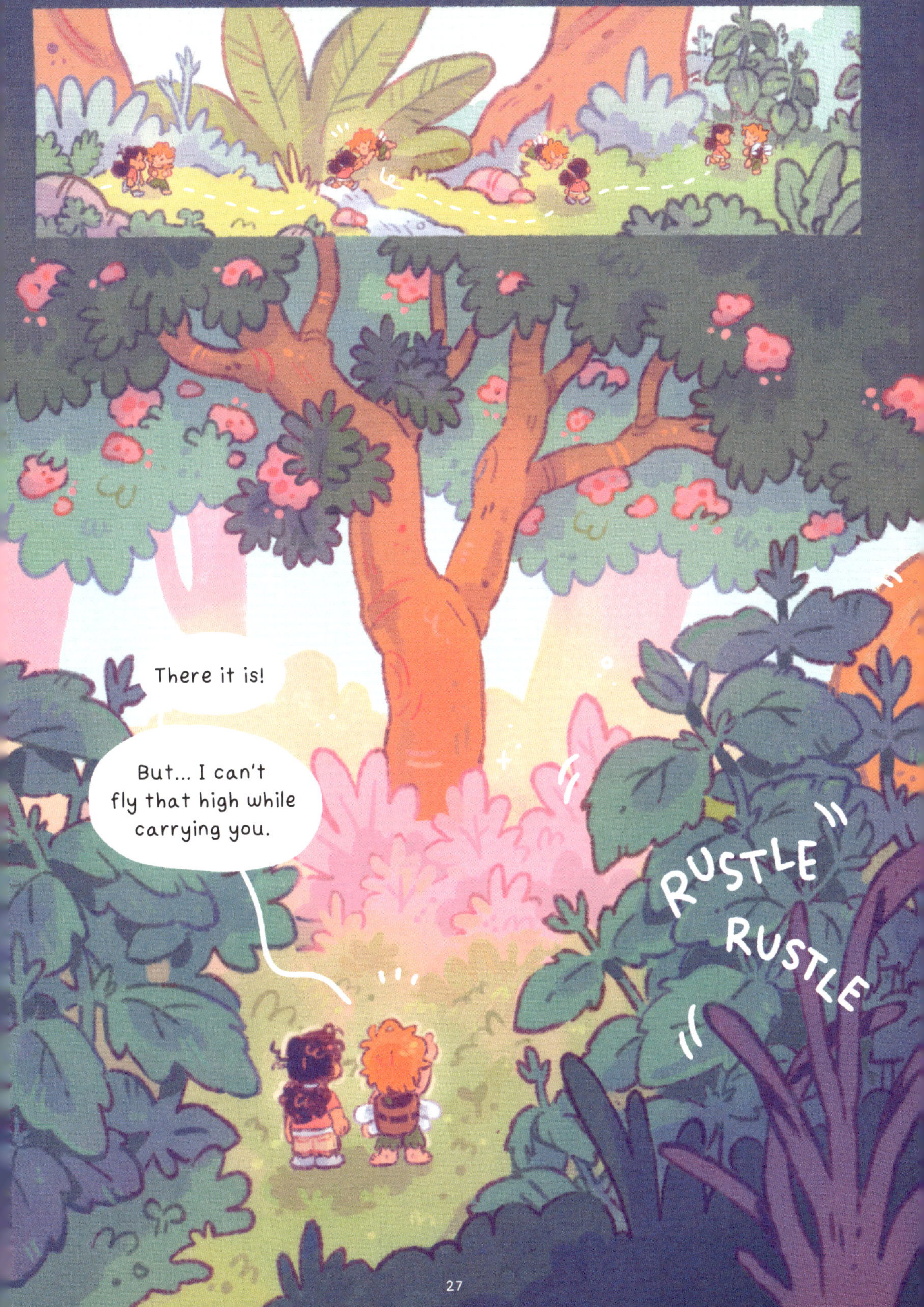
There it is!
But... I can't fly that high while carrying you.
RUSTLE
RUSTLE

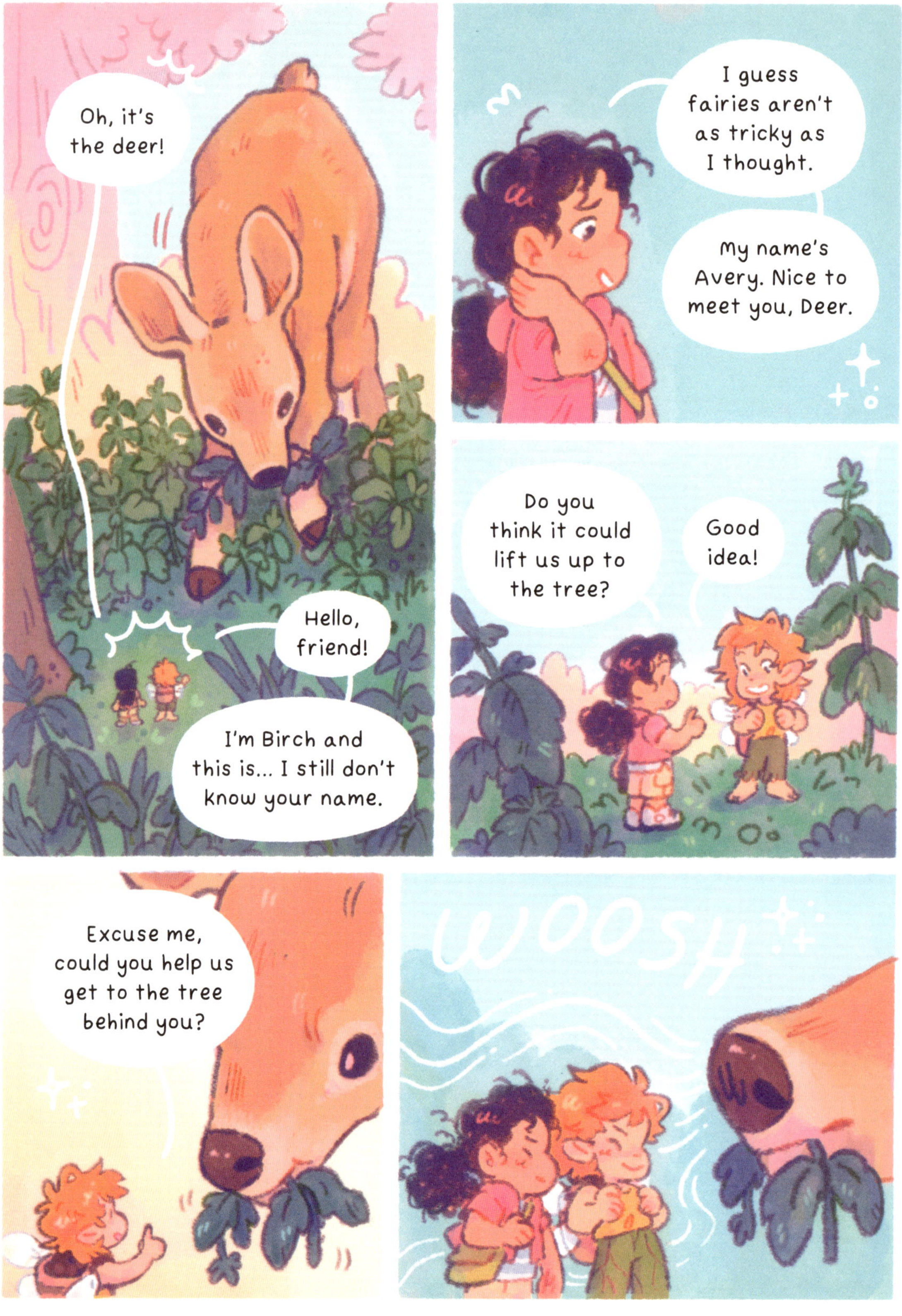

Oh, it's the deer!
Hello, friend!
I'm Birch and this is... I still don't know your name.
I guess fairies aren't as tricky as I thought.
My name's Avery. Nice to meet you, Deer.
Do you think it could lift us up to the tree?
Good idea!
Excuse me, could you help us get to the tree behind you?
WOOSH

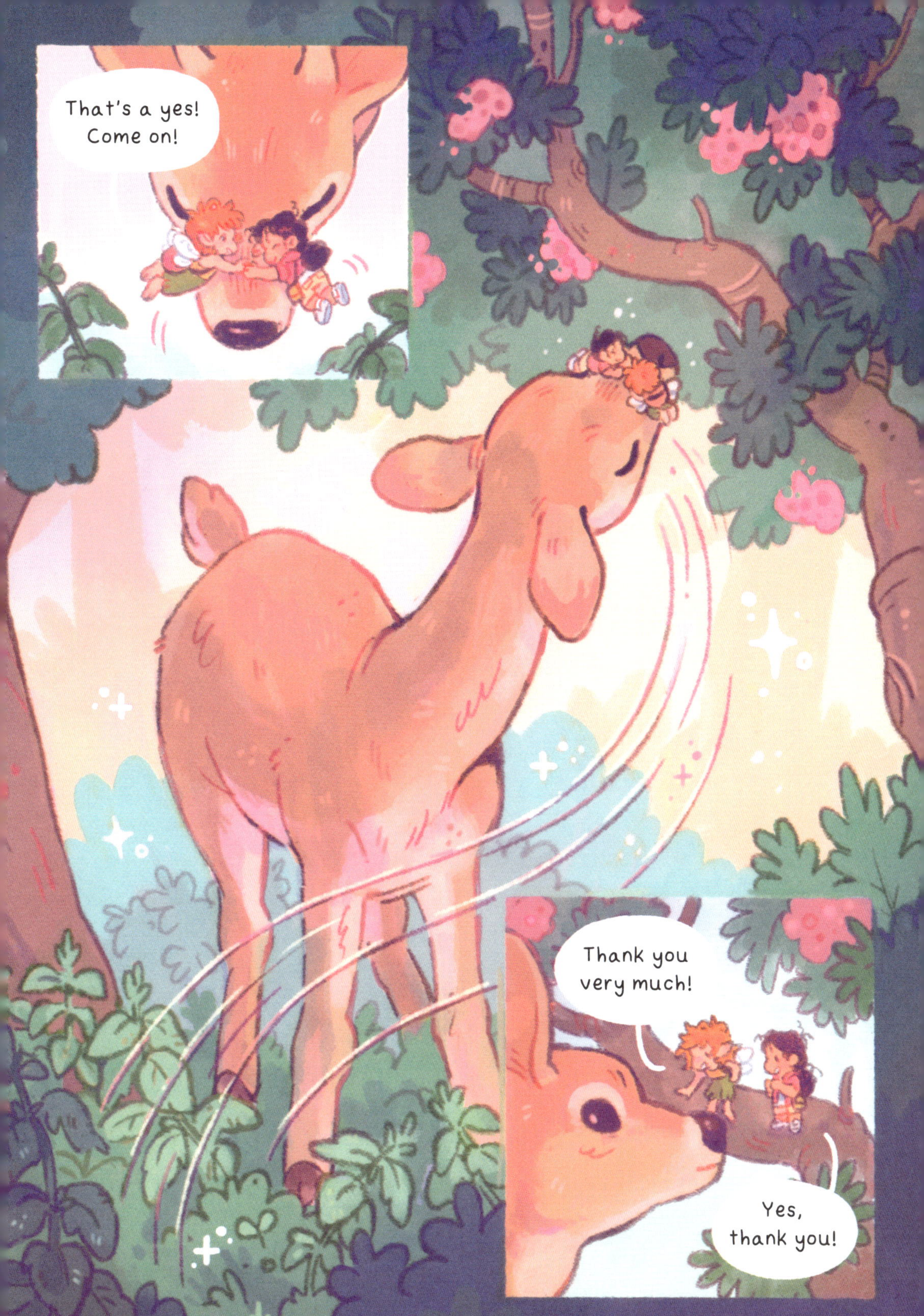
That's a yes! Come on!
Thank you very much!
Yes, thank you!

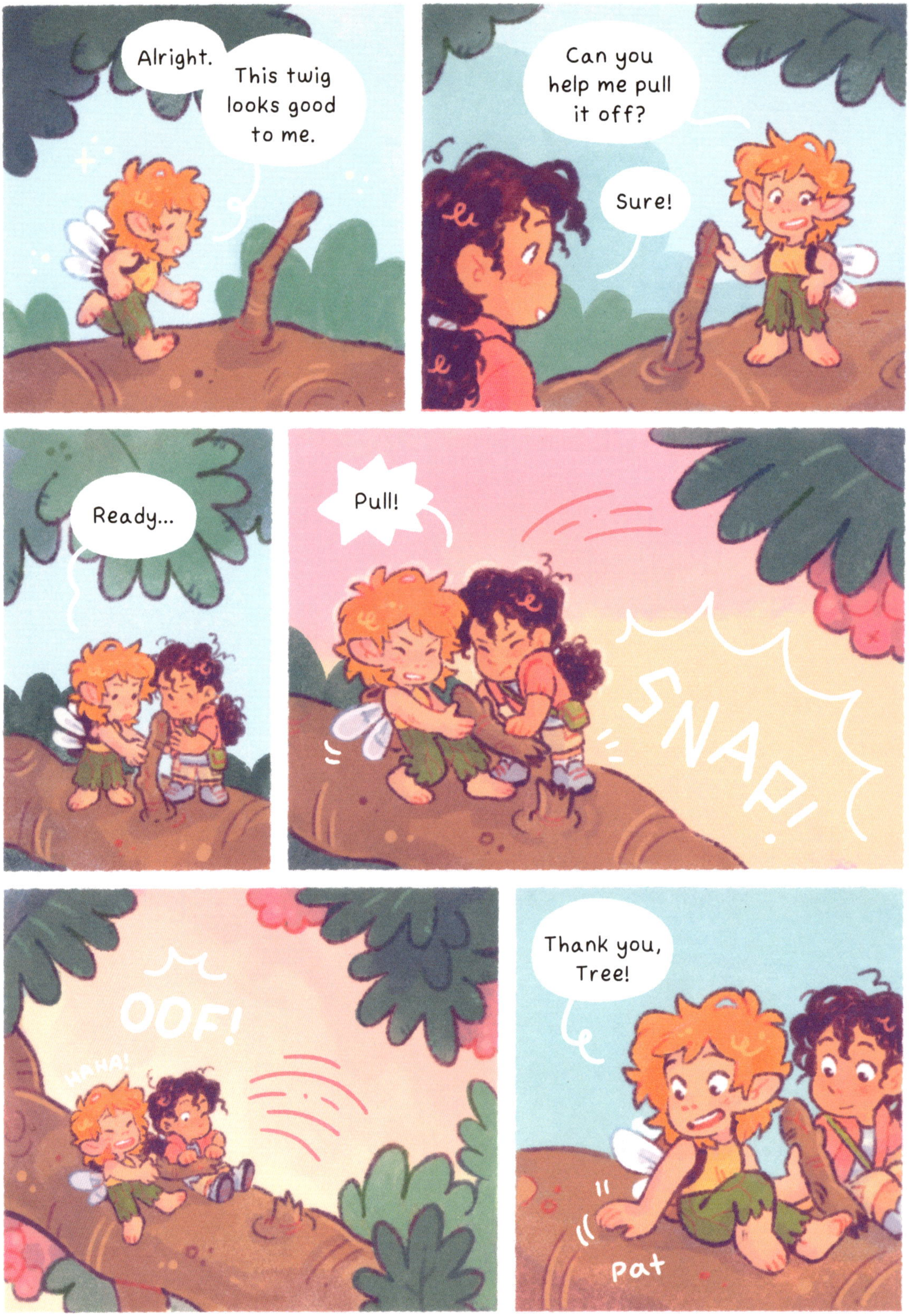
Alright.
This twig looks good to me.
Can you help me pull it off?
Sure!
Ready...
Pull!
SNAP!
OOF!
HAHA!
Thank you, Tree!
Pat

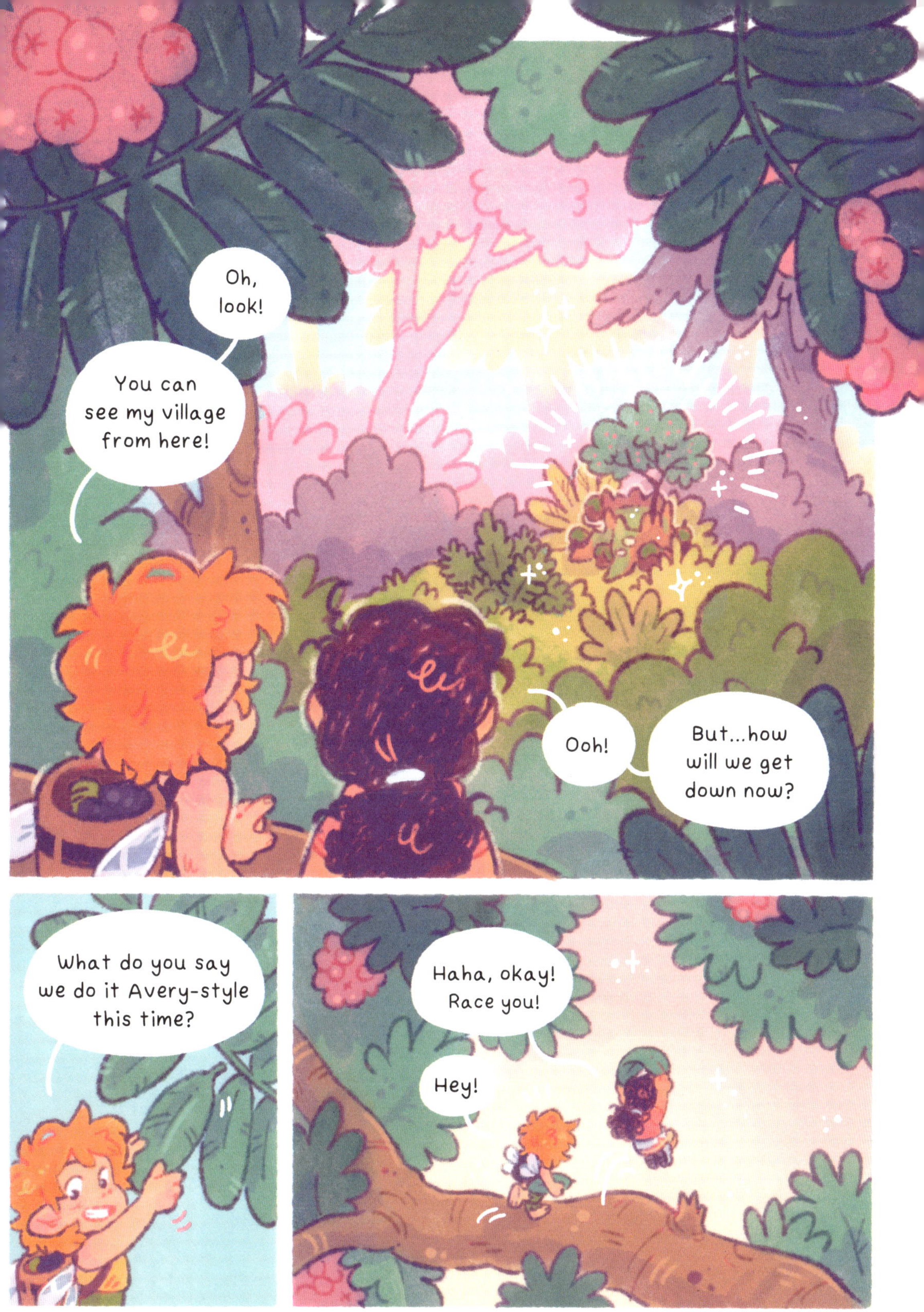
Oh, look!
You can see my village from here!
Ooh!
But...how will we get down now?
What do you say we do it Avery-style this time?
Haha, okay! Race you!
Hey!

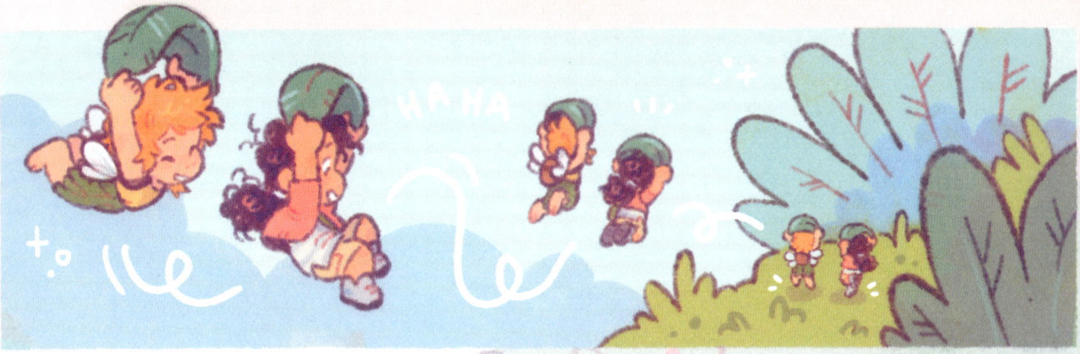
HAHA

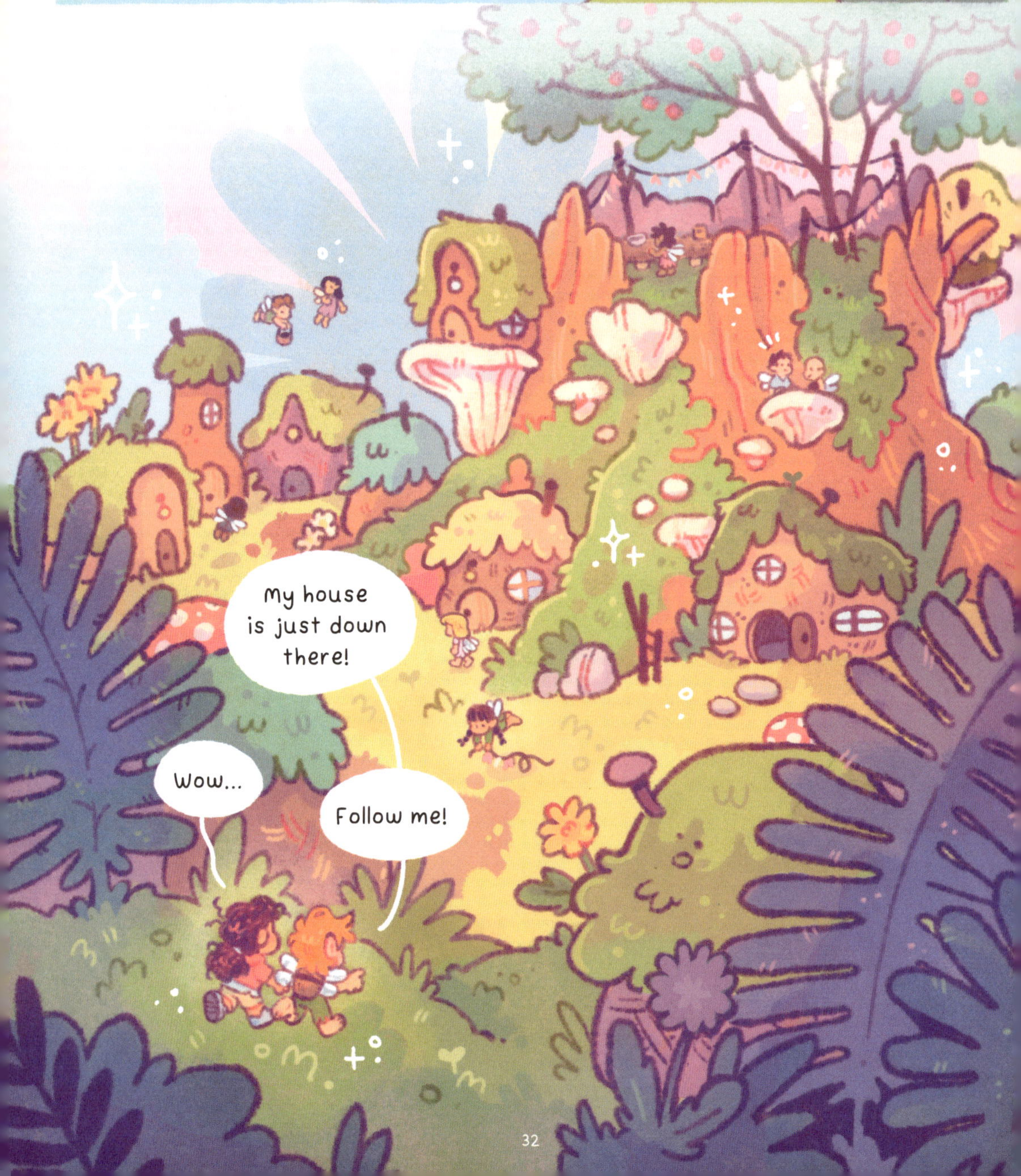
My house is just down there!
Wow...
Follow me!

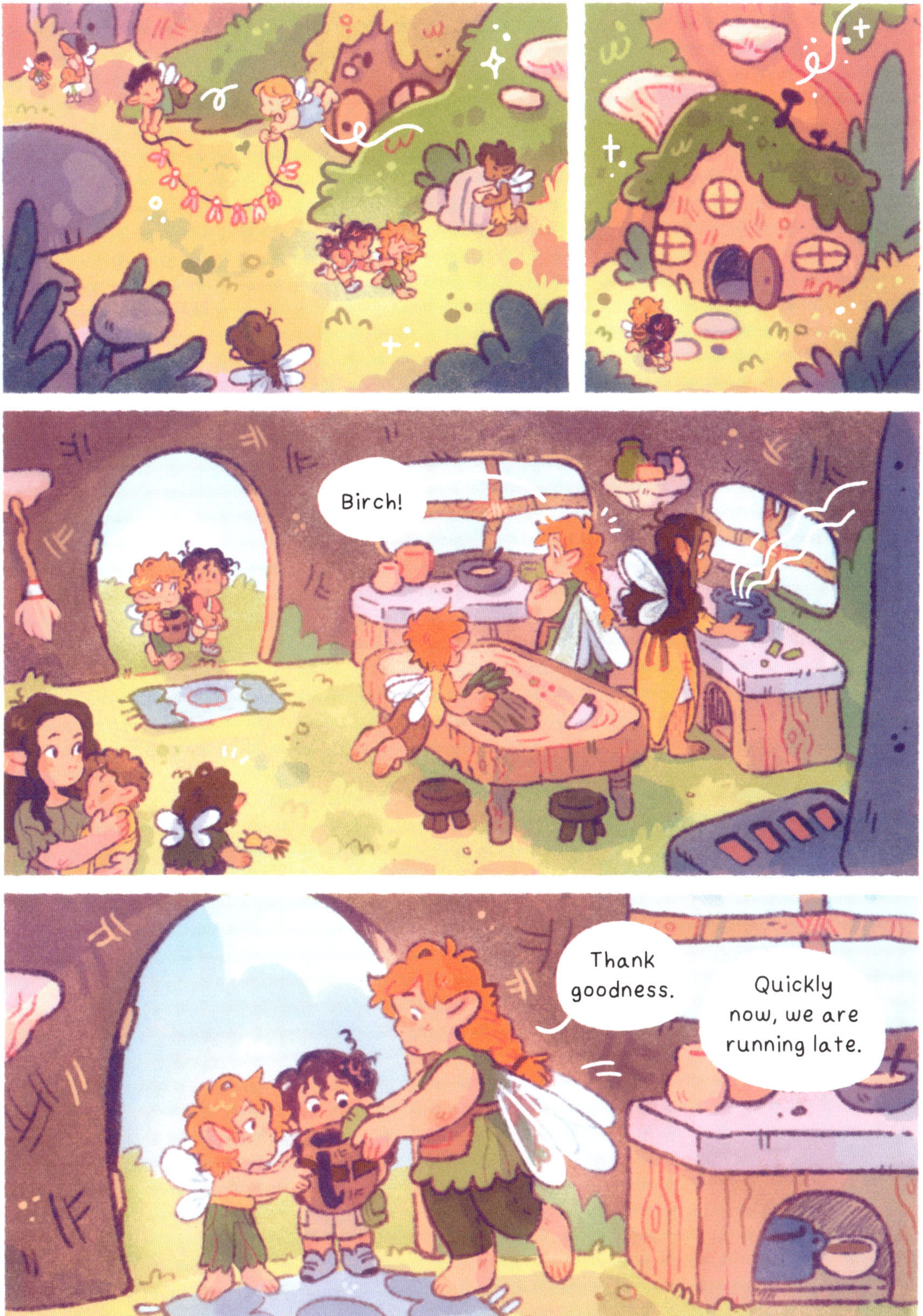
Birch!
Thank goodness.
Quickly now, we are running late.

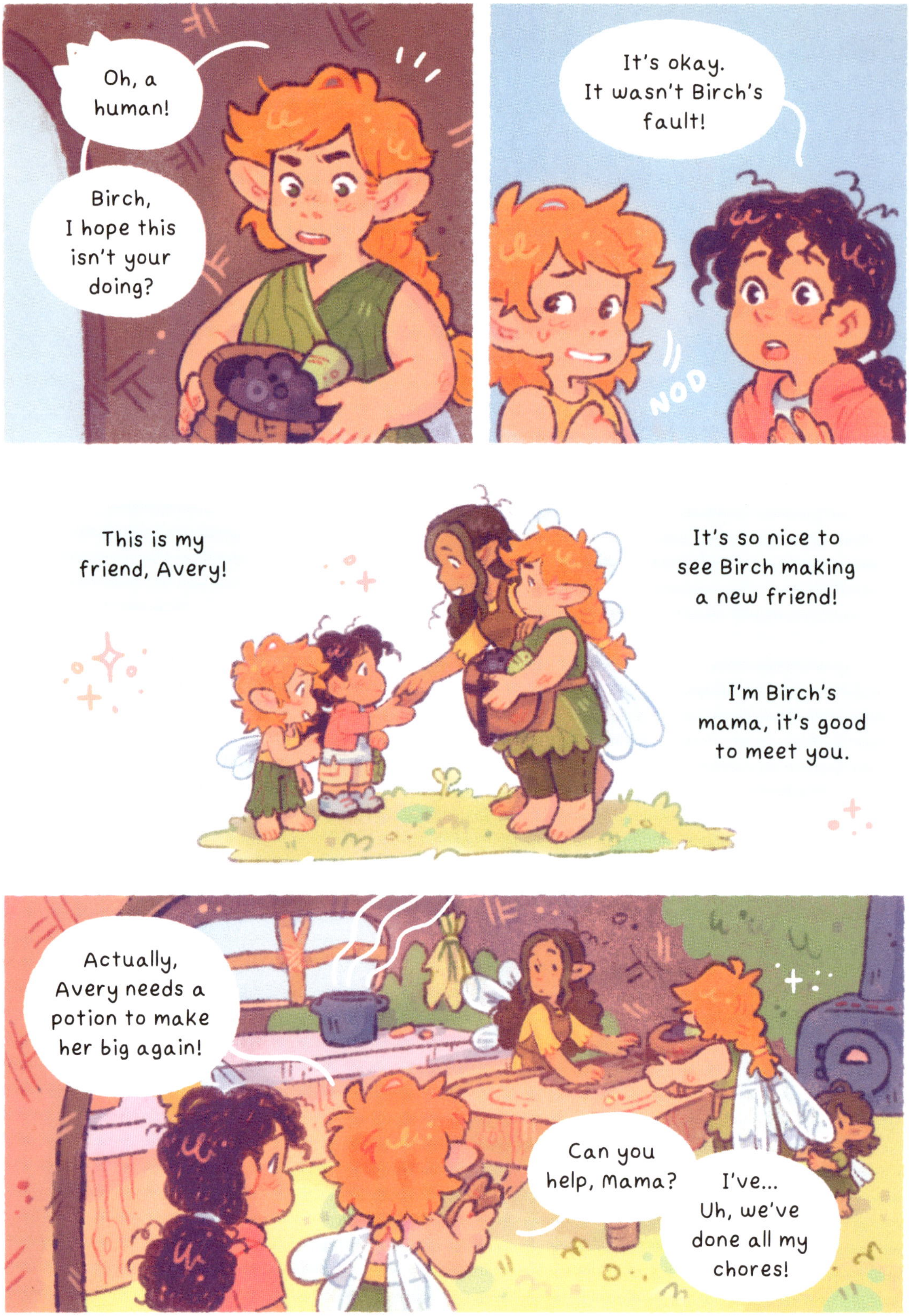
Oh, a human!
Birch, I hope this isn't your doing?
It's okay. It wasn't Birch's fault!
NOD
This is my friend, Avery!
It's so nice to see Birch making a new friend!
I'm Birch's mama, it's good to meet you.
Actually, Avery needs a potion to make her big again!
Can you help, Mama?
I've... Uh, we've done all my chores!

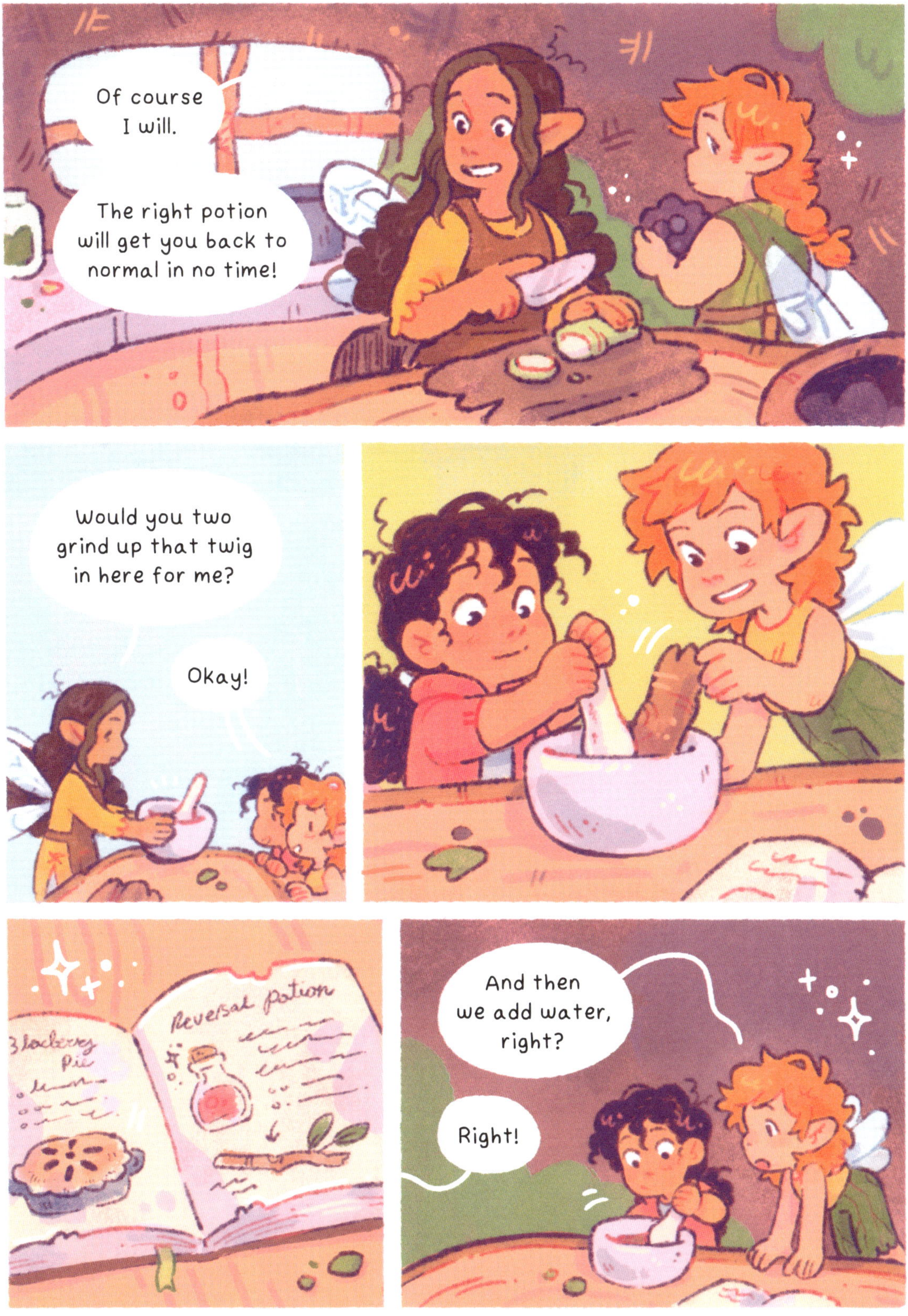

Of course I will.
The right potion will get you back to normal in no time!
Would you two grind up that twig in here for me?
Okay!
Reversal potion
And then we add water, right?
Right!

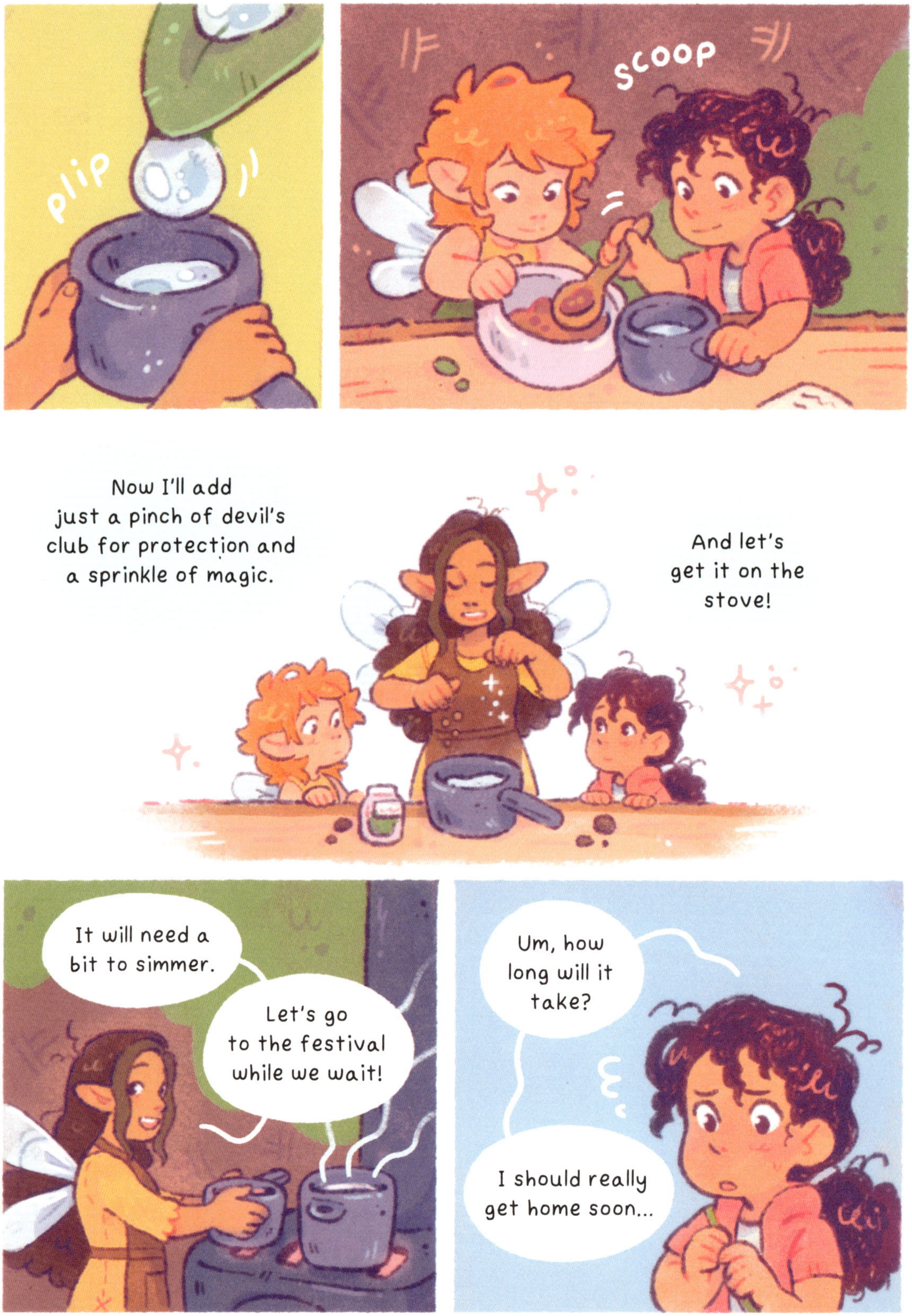
plip
scoop
Now I'll add just a pinch of devil's club for protection and a sprinkle of magic.
And let's get it on the stove!
It will need a bit to simmer.
Let's go to the festival while we wait!
Um, how long will it take?
I should really get home soon...

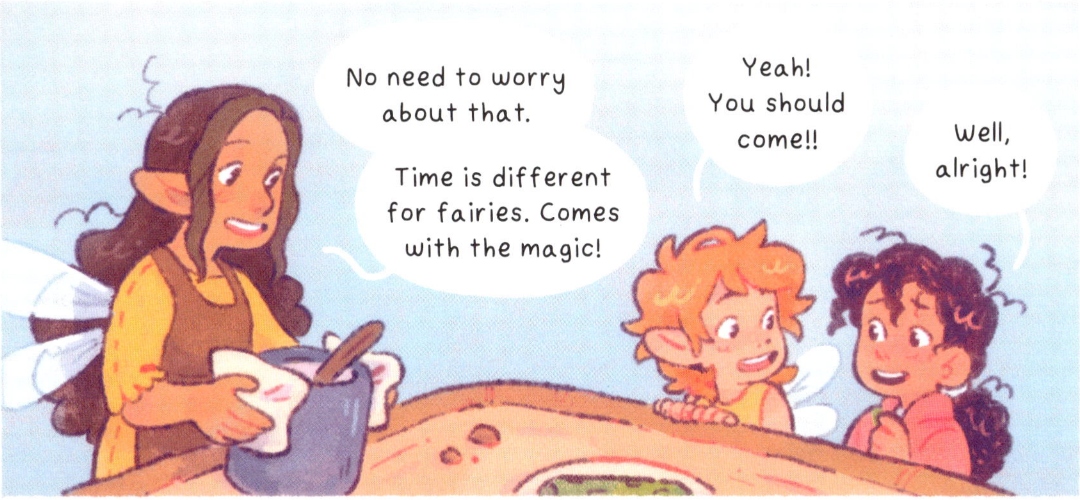
No need to worry about that.
Time is different for fairies. Comes with the magic!
Yeah! You should come!!
Well, alright!

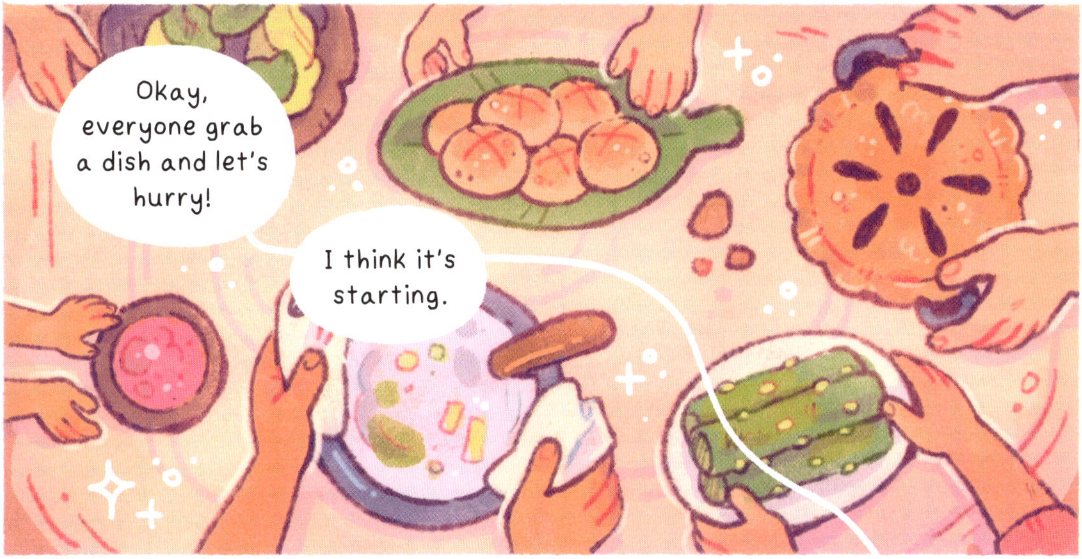
Okay, everyone grab a dish and let's hurry!
I think it's starting.

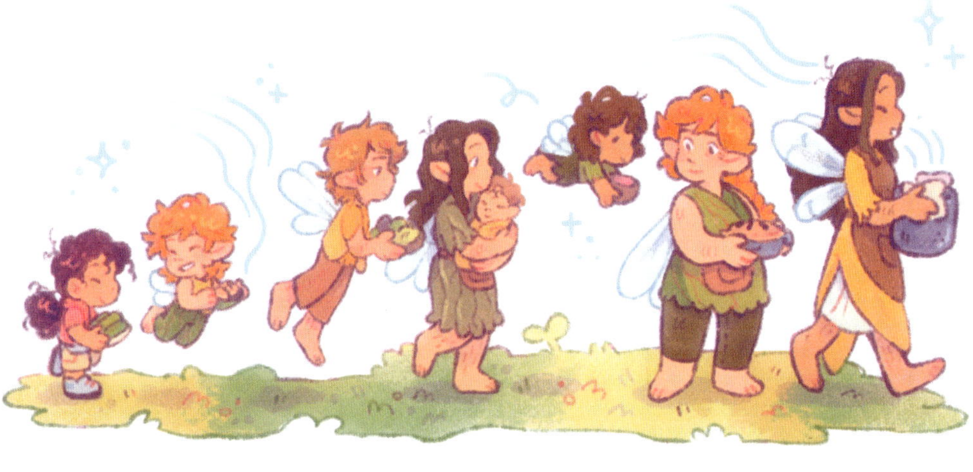

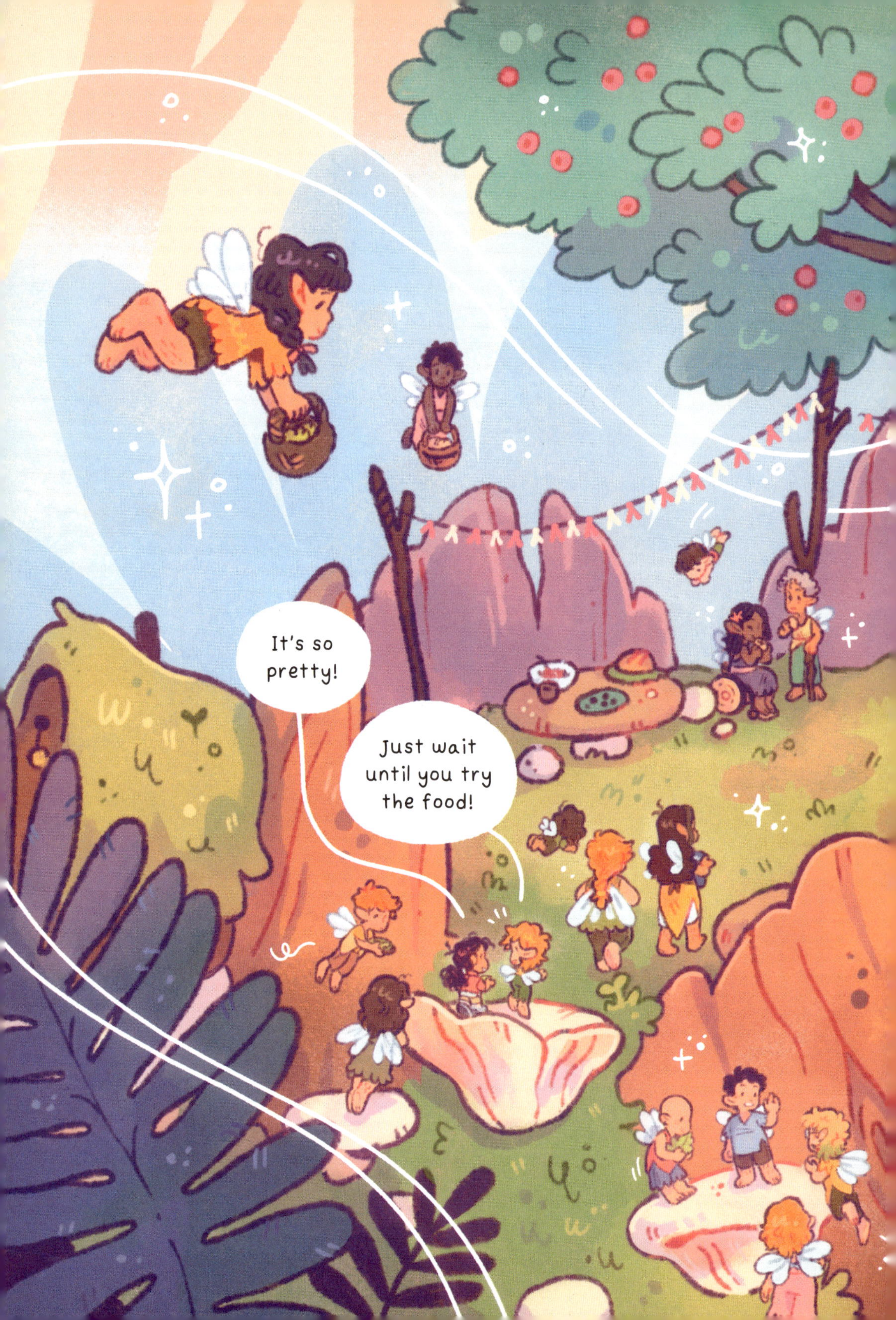
It's so pretty!
Just wait until you try the food!

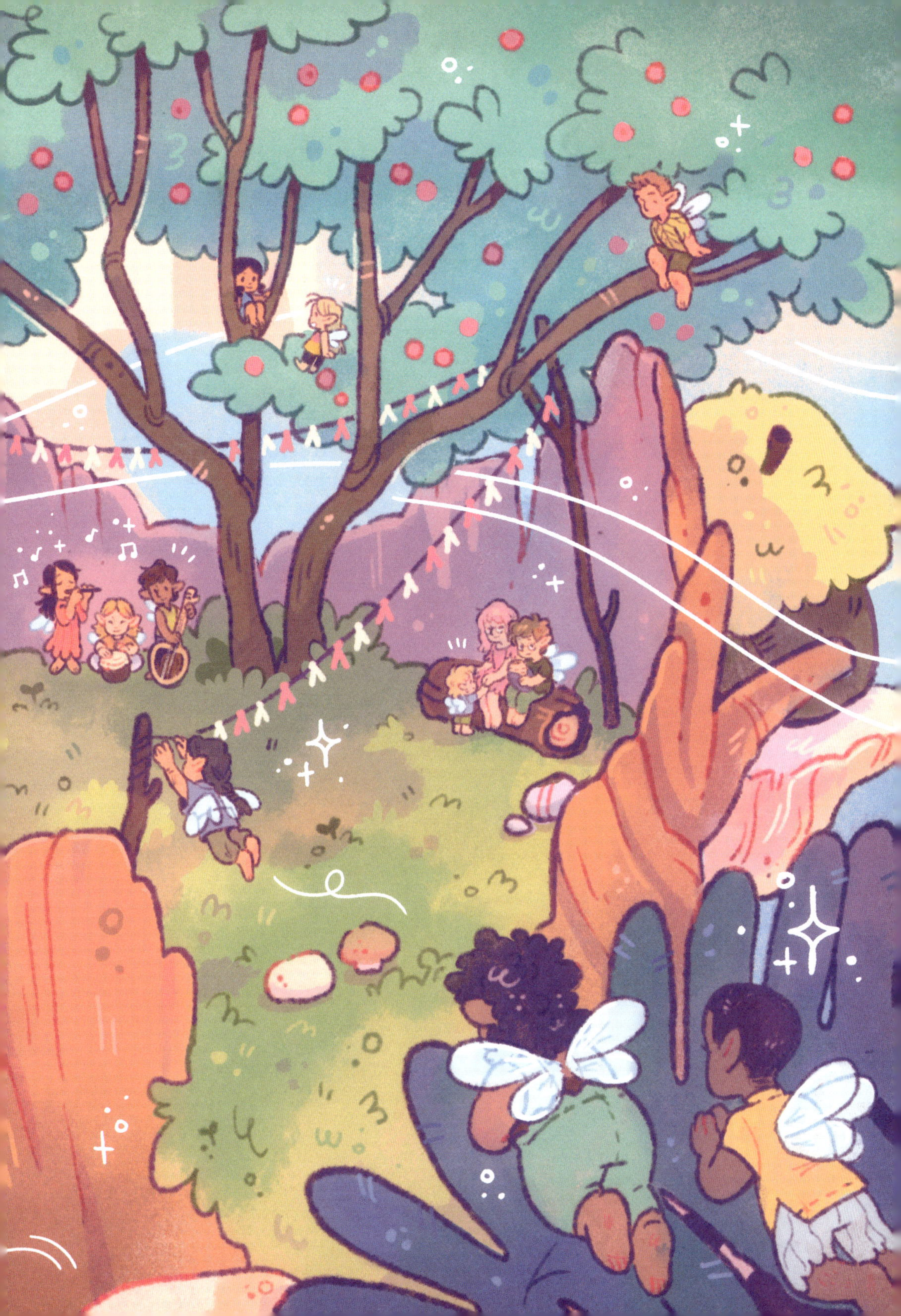

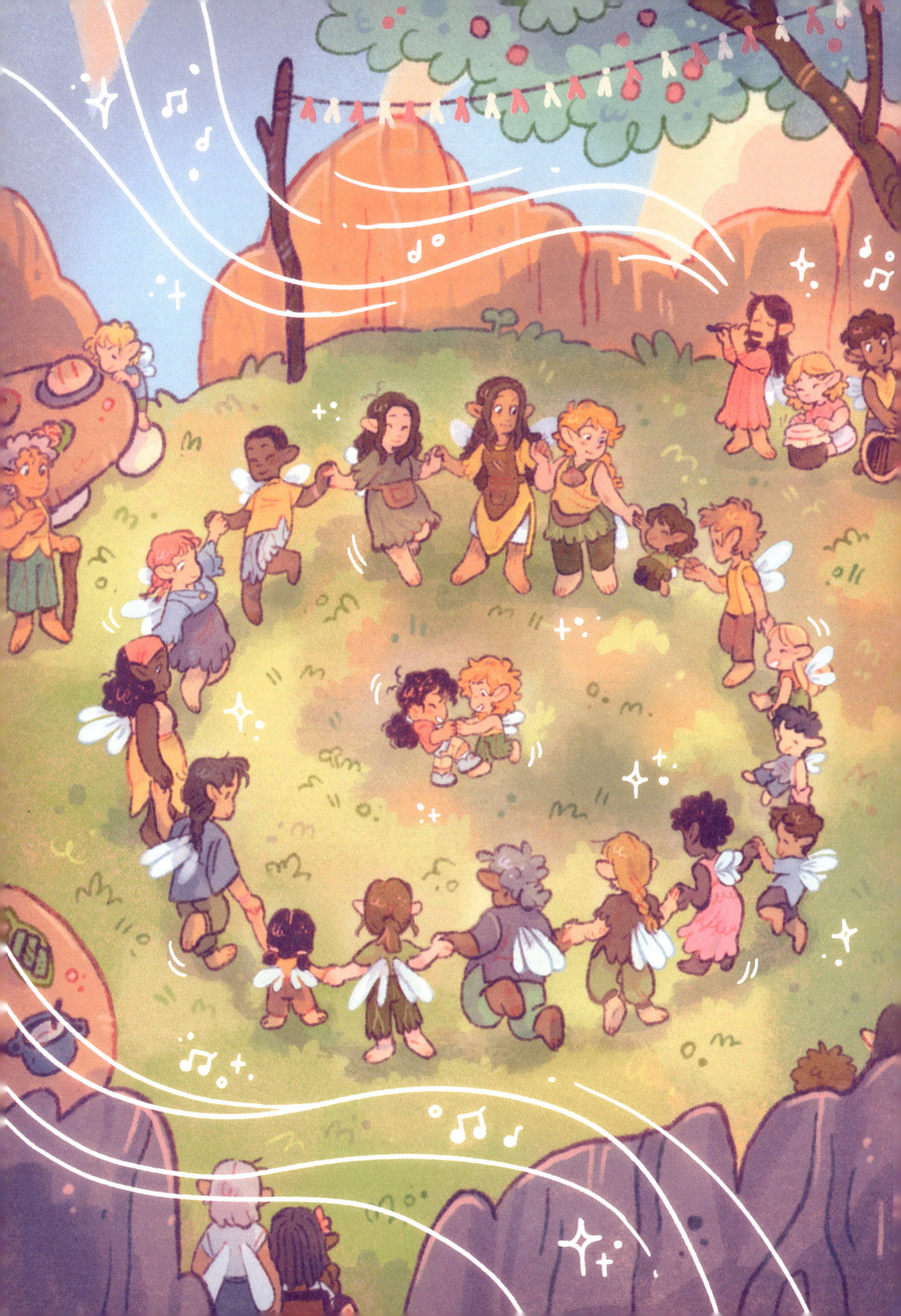

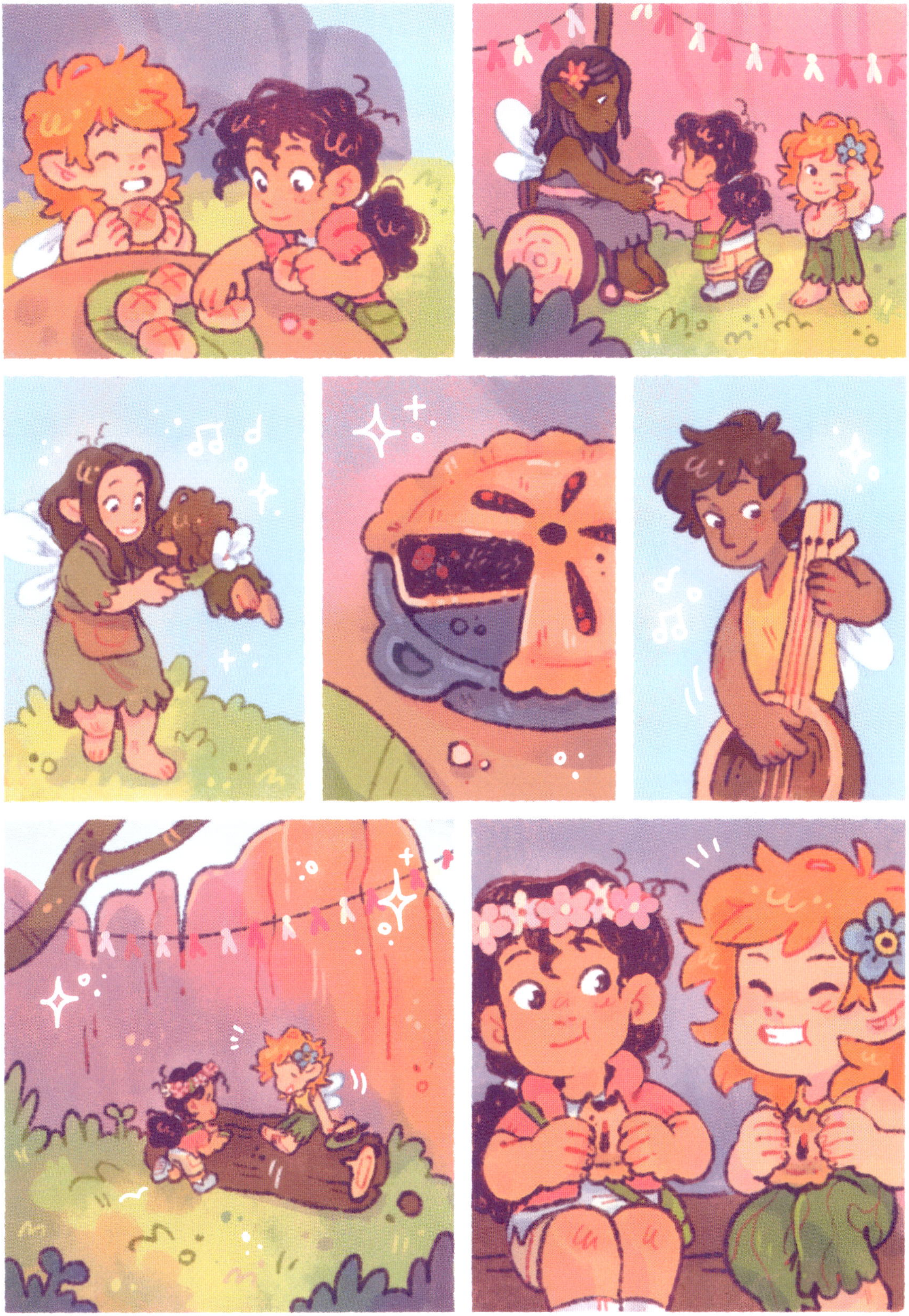

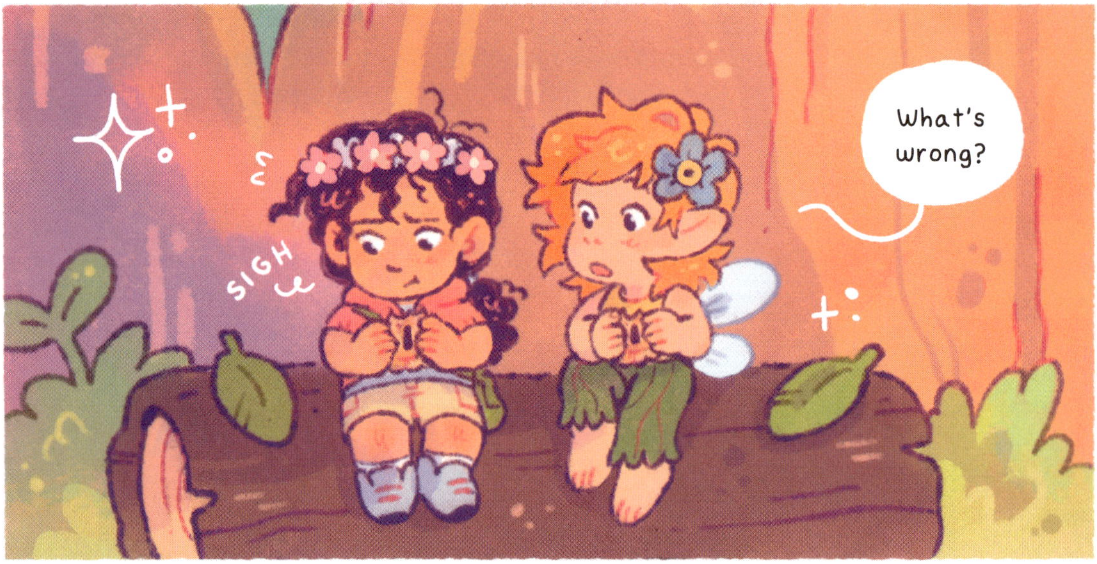
SIGH
What's wrong?

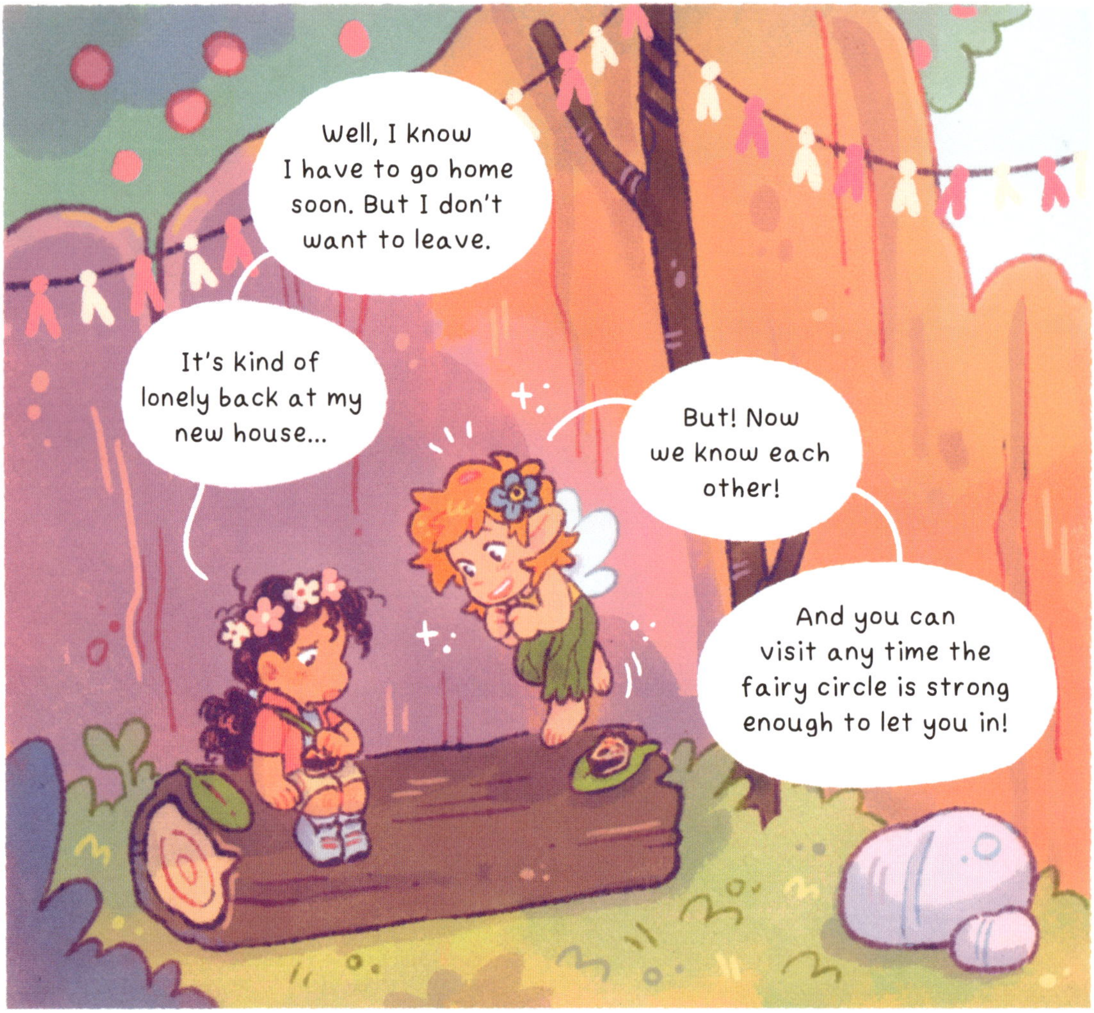
Well, I know I have to go home soon. But I don't want to leave.
It's kind of lonely back at my new house...
But! Now we know each other!
And you can visit any time the fairy circle is strong enough to let you in!

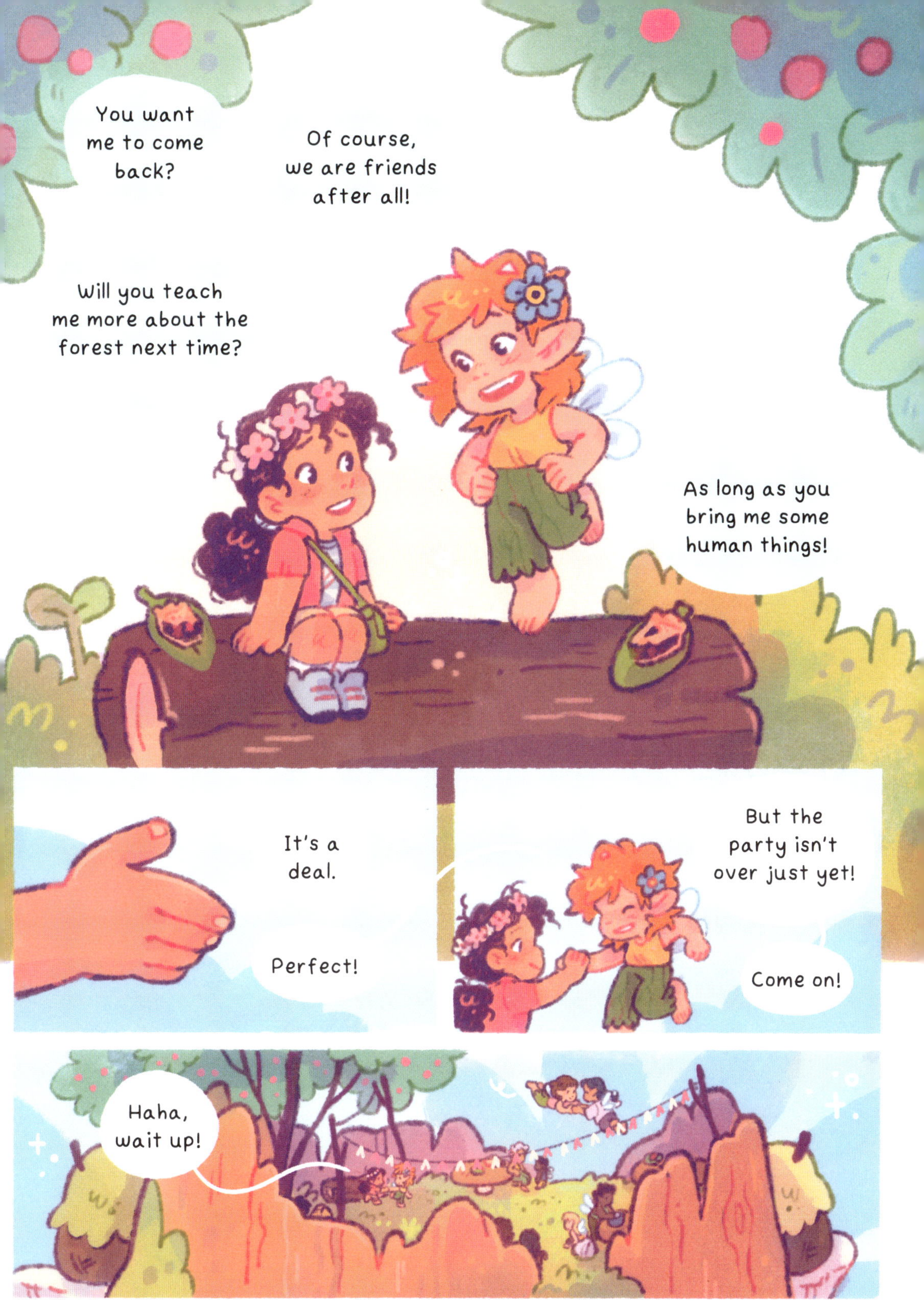

You want me to come back?
Of course, we are friends after all!
Will you teach me more about the forest next time?
As long as you bring me some human things!
It's a deal.
Perfect!
But the party isn't over just yet!
Come on!
Haha, wait up!

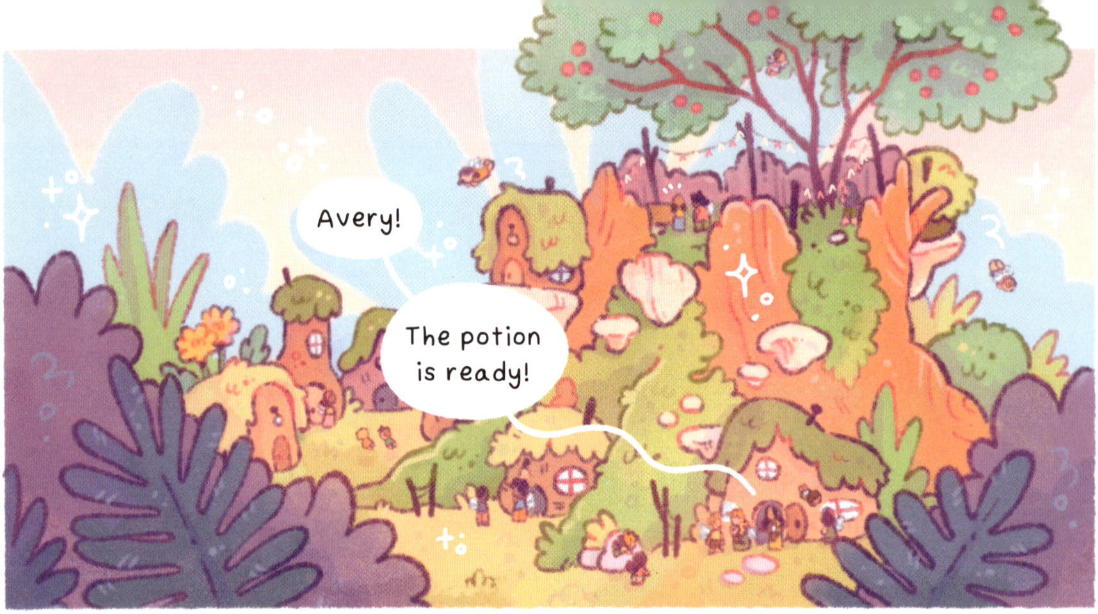
Avery!
The potion is ready!

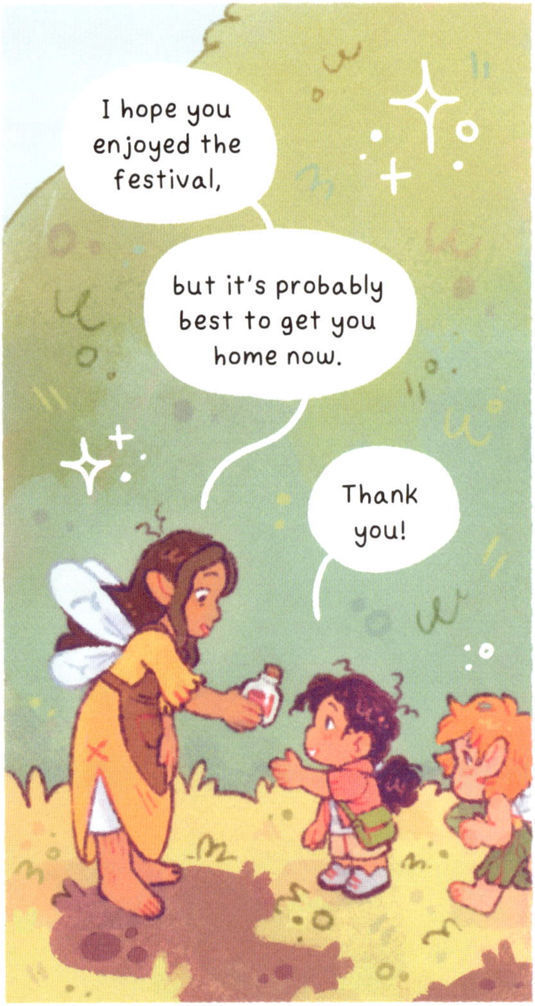
I hope you enjoyed the festival,
but it's probably best to get you home now.
Thank you!

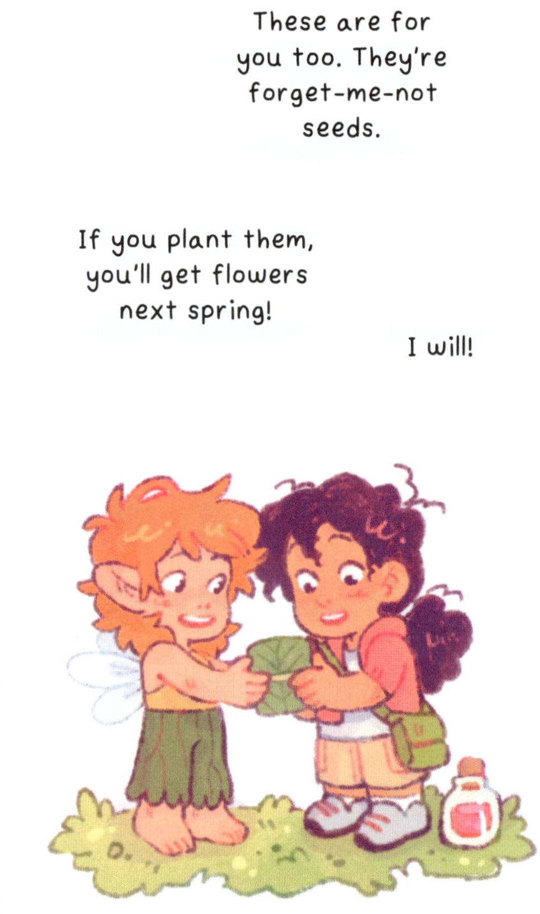
These are for you too. They're forget-me-not seeds.
If you plant them, you'll get flowers next spring!
I will!

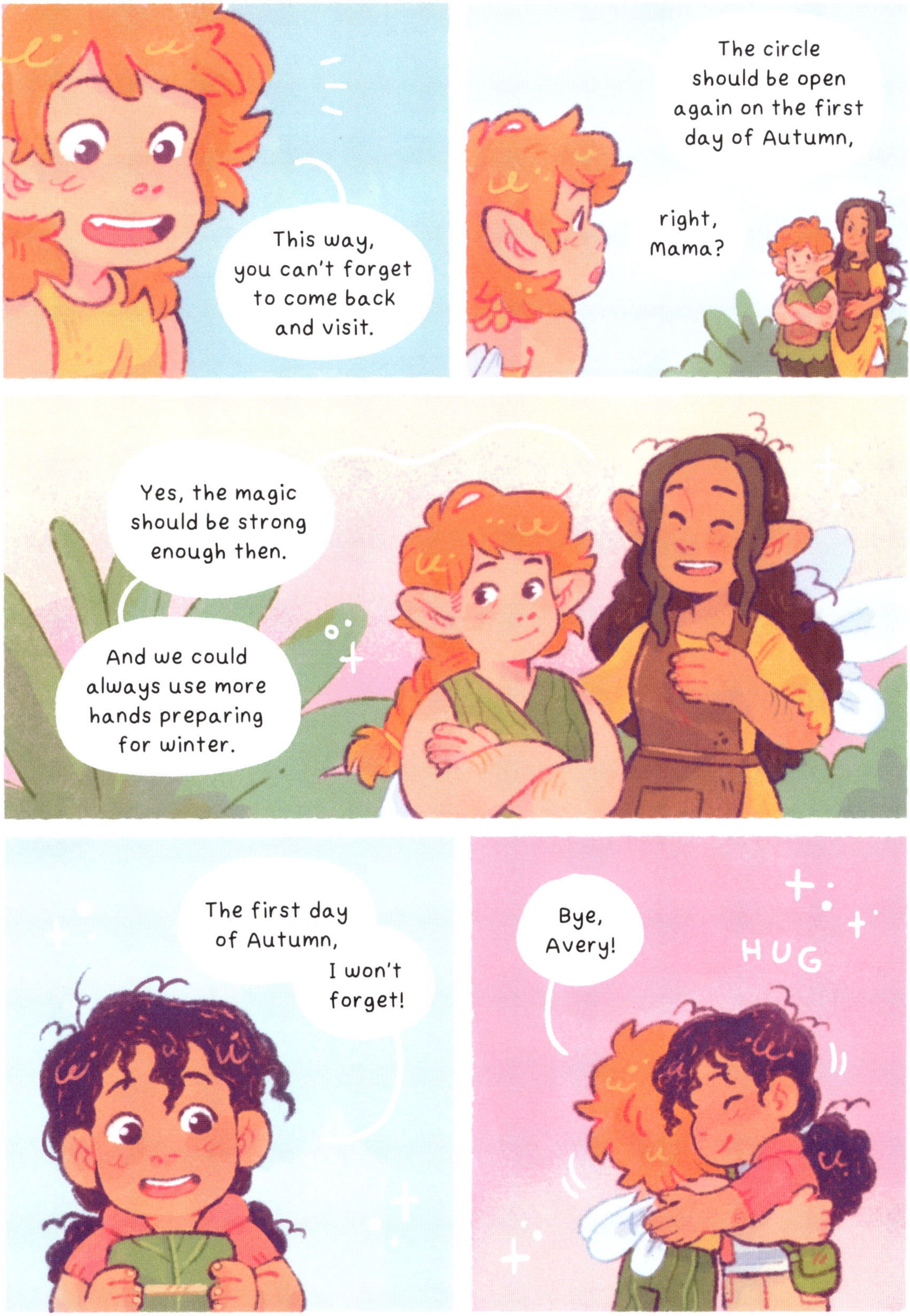
This way, you can't forget to come back and visit.
The circle should be open again on the first day of Autumn,
right, Mama?
Yes, the magic should be strong enough then.
And we could always use more hands preparing for winter.
The first day of Autumn,
I won't forget!
Bye, Avery!
HUG

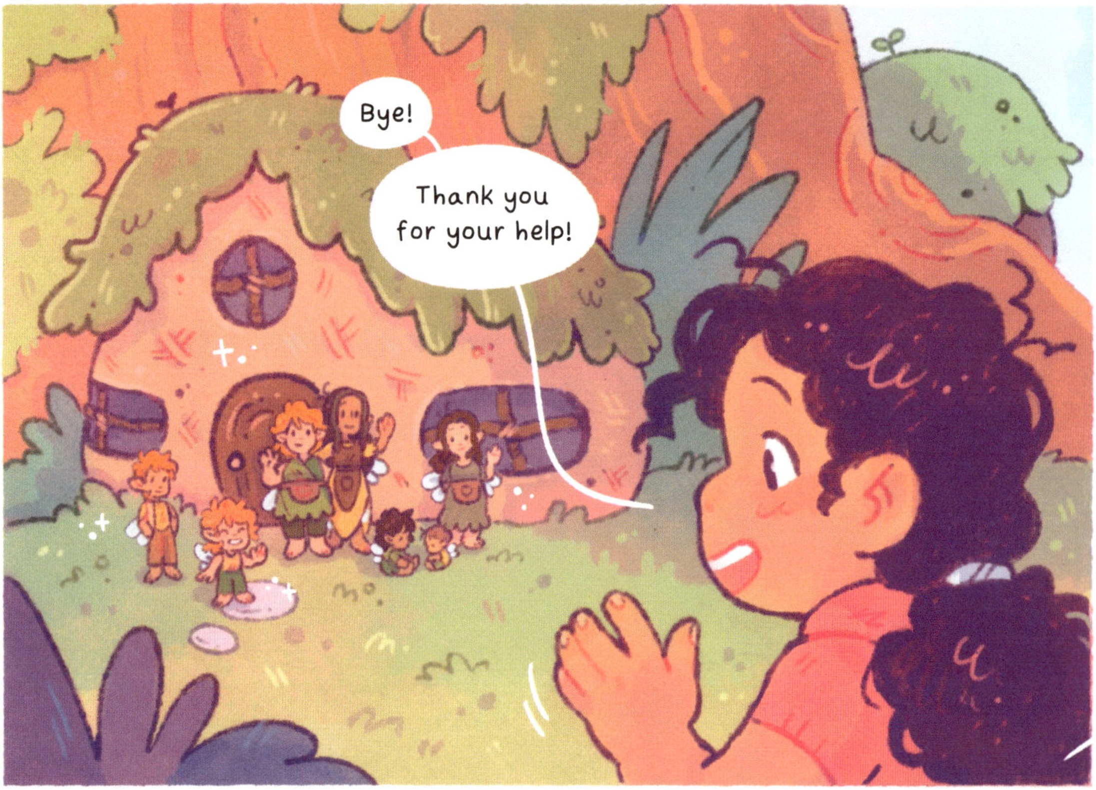
Bye!
Thank you for your help!

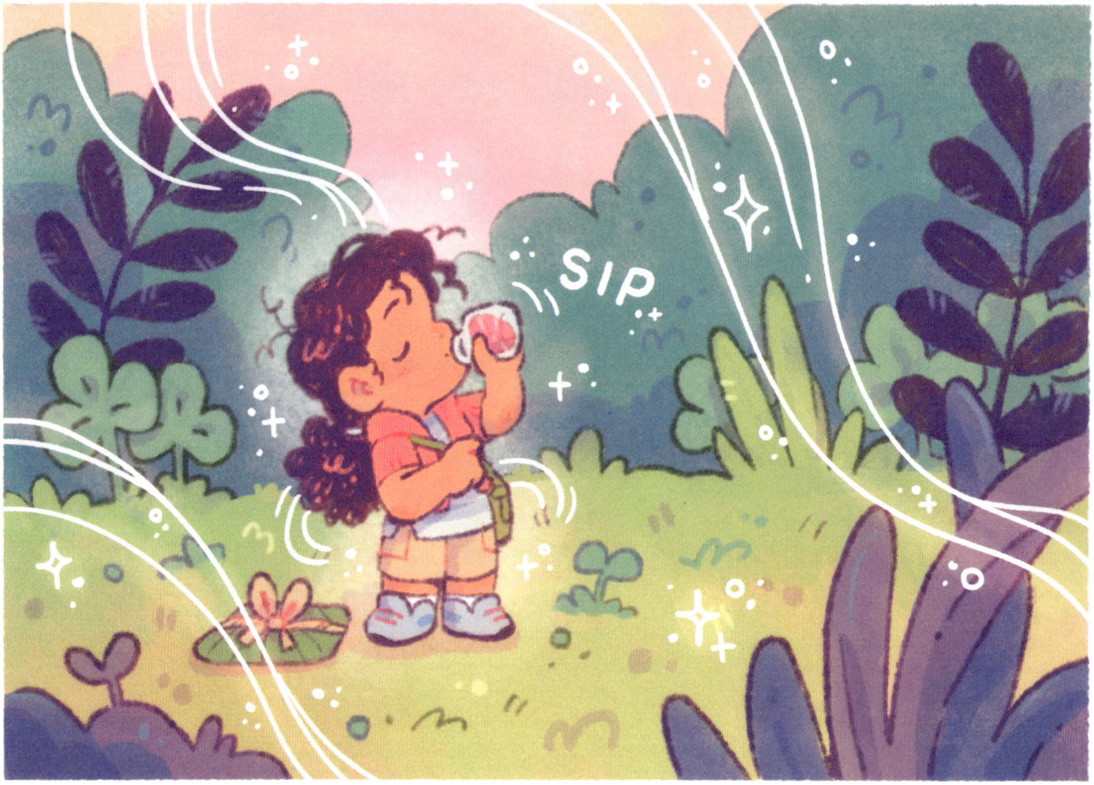
SIP

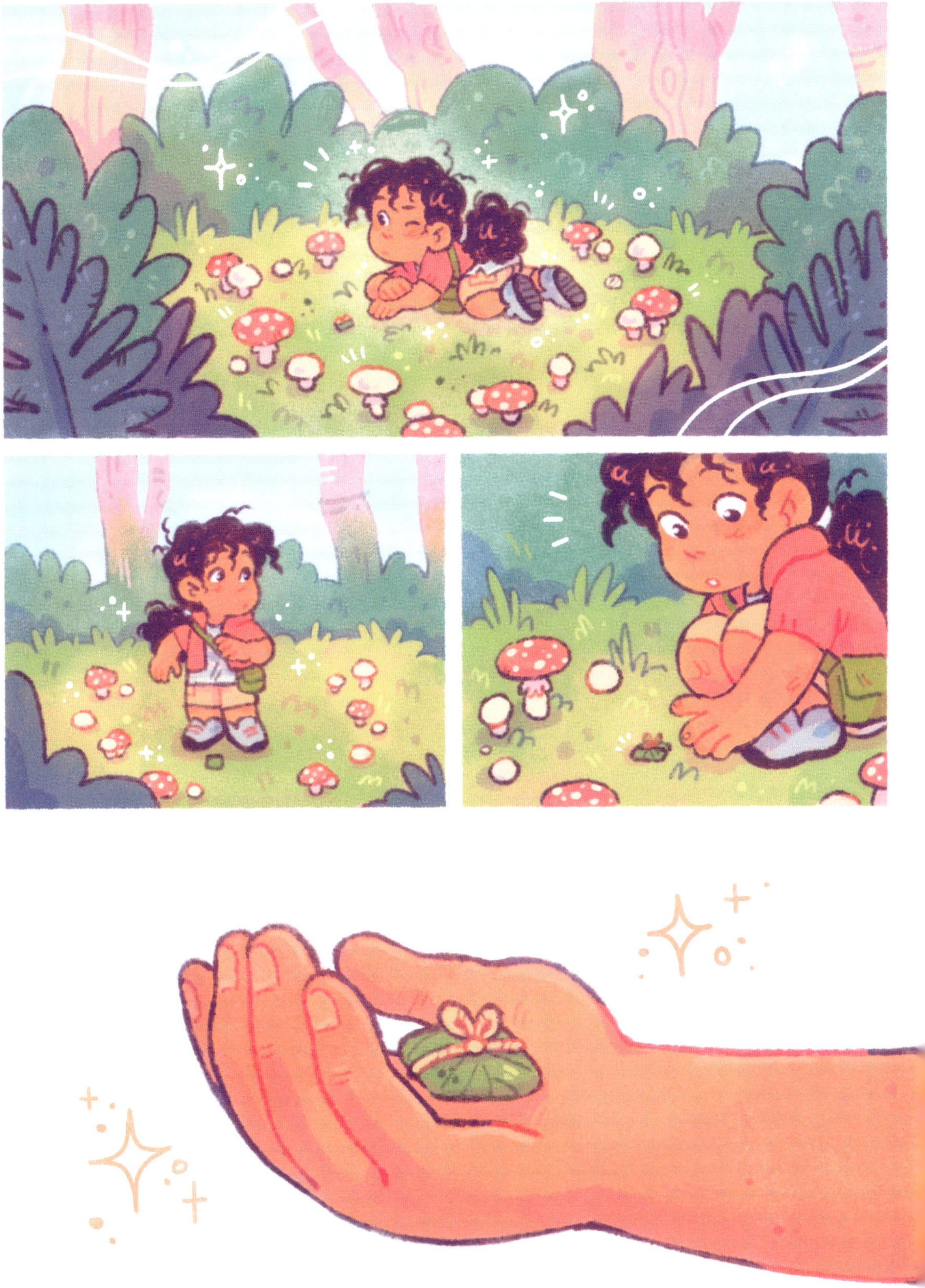

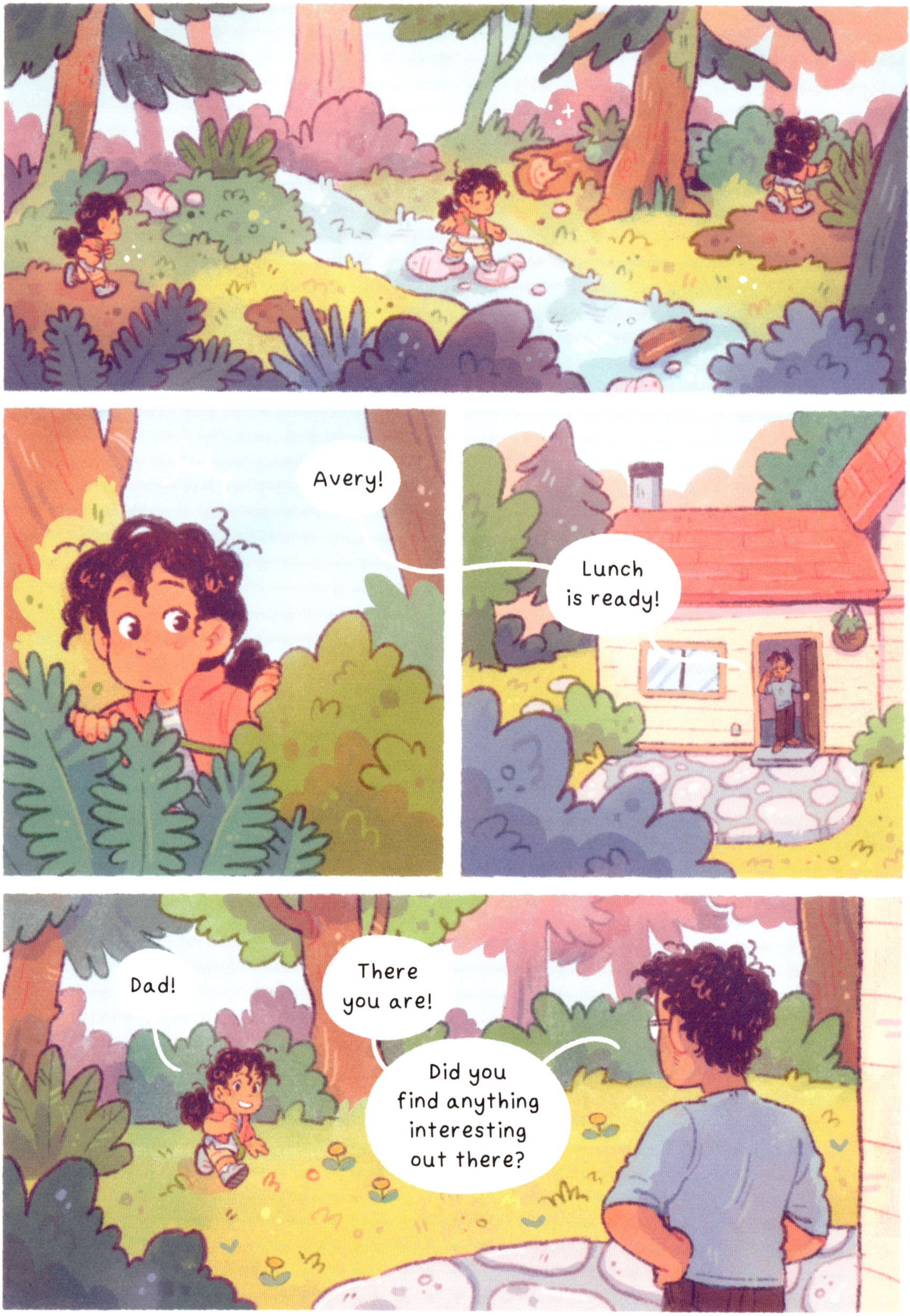
Avery!
Lunch is ready!
Dad!
There you are!
Did you find anything interesting out there?

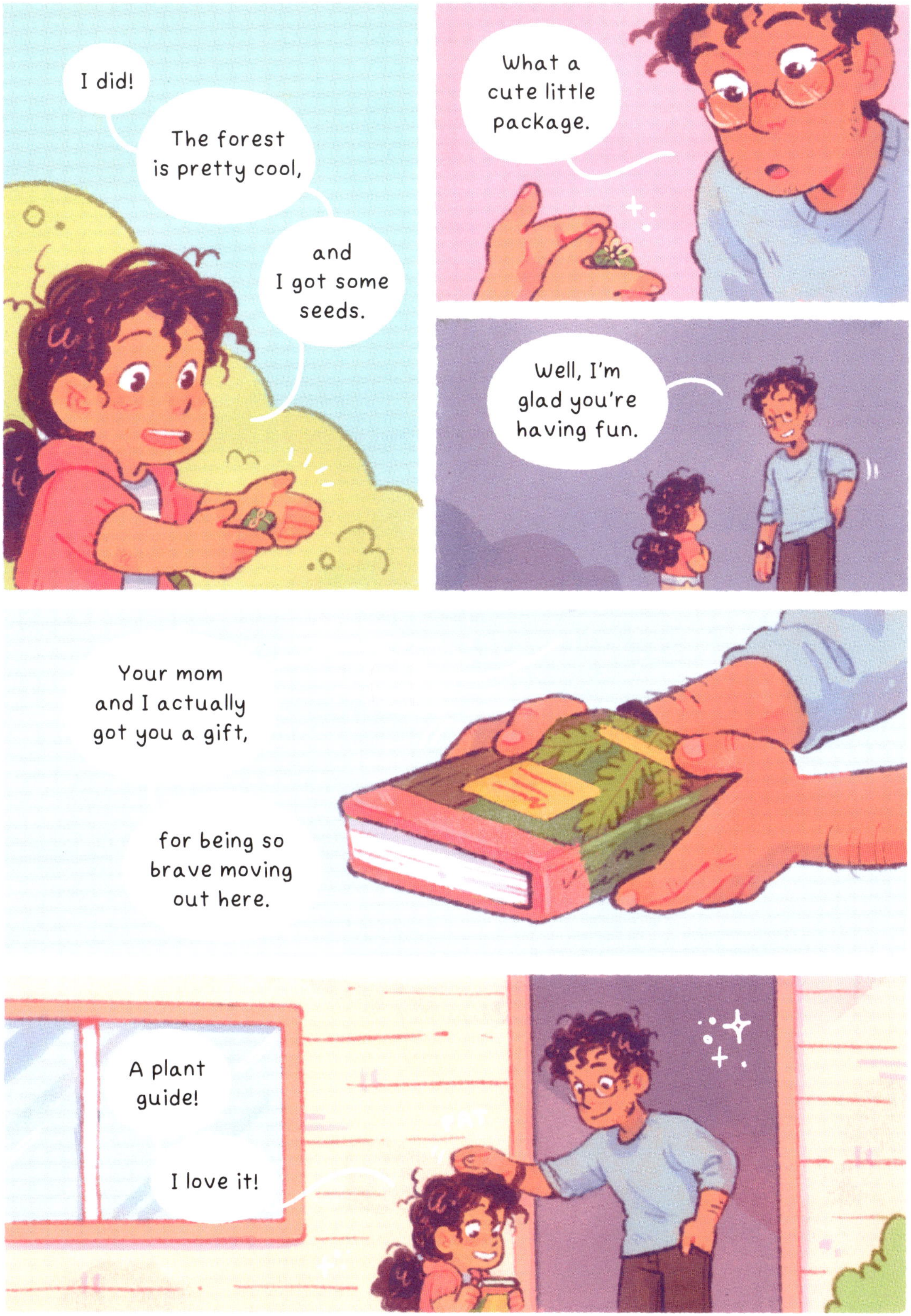
I did!
The forest is pretty cool,
and I got some seeds.
What a cute little package.
Well, I'm glad you're having fun.
Your mom and I actually got you a gift,
for being so brave moving out here.
A plant guide!
I love it!

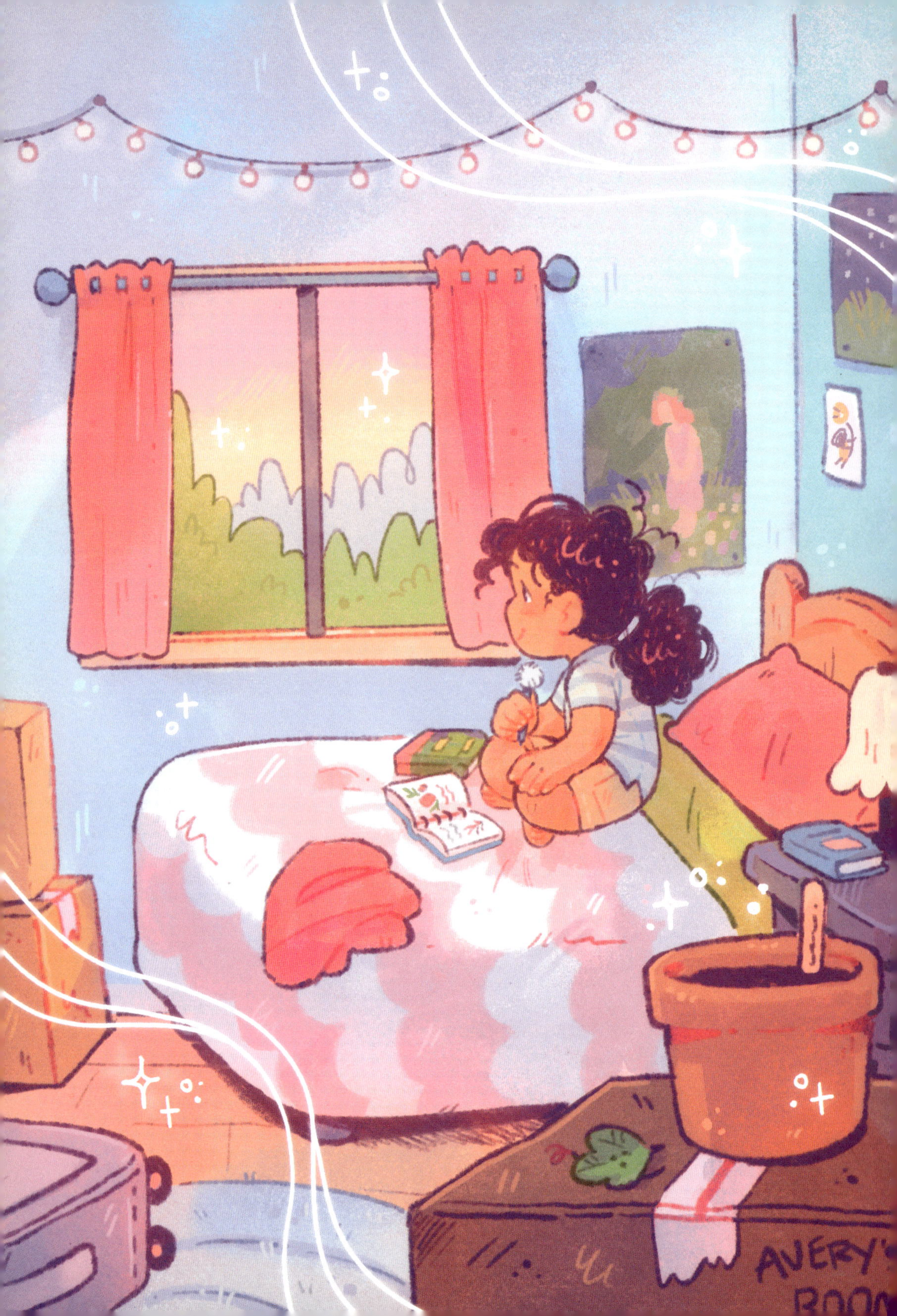
AVERY'

6/21 - Today I found all sorts of new things in the forest AND made a new friend! I've decided I want to learn about all the plants in the forest so I can make my own plant guide someday.

TODAY'S DISCOVERIES

Licorice Fern

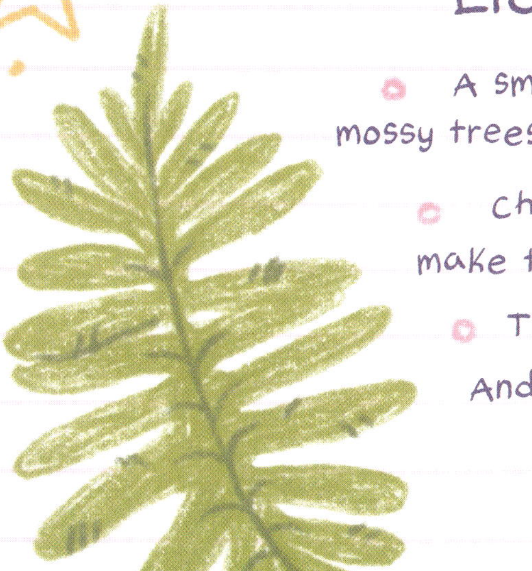

- A small fern found on mossy trees, logs, and rocks.
- Chew on the roots or make them into tea.
- Tastes like licorice! And dirt...

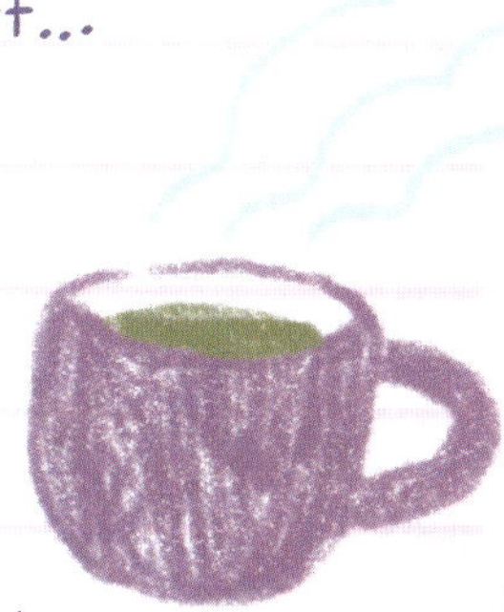

LICORICE ROOT TEA!

Blackberries

A spiky shrub full of delicious berries!

Related to raspberries and salmonberries.

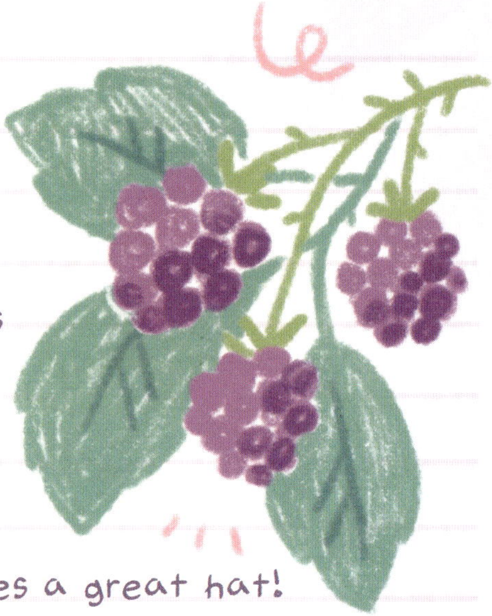

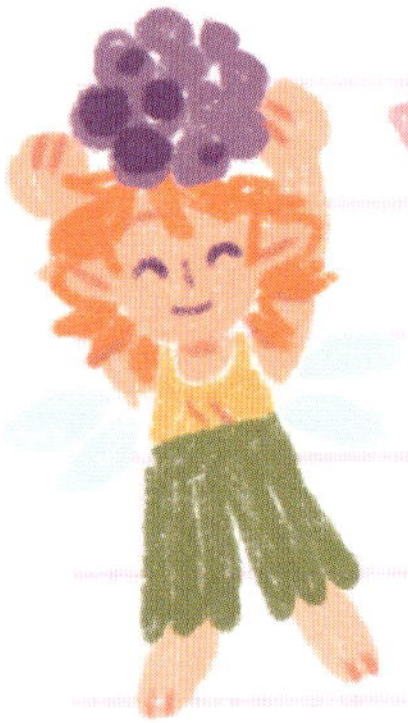

Makes a great hat!

Mountain Ash

Also known as a "Rowan tree."

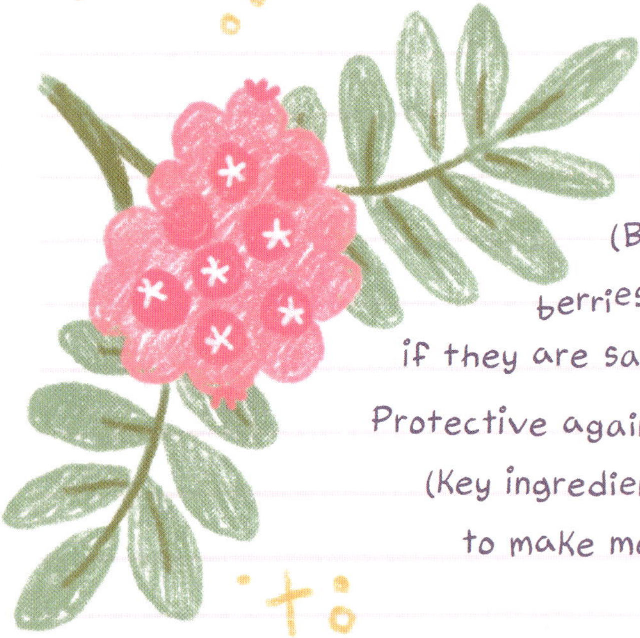

Birds love to eat the red berries it grows!

(But never eat berries if you don't know if they are safe for humans!)

Protective against magic

(Key ingredient in the potion to make me big again!)

FAIRIES!

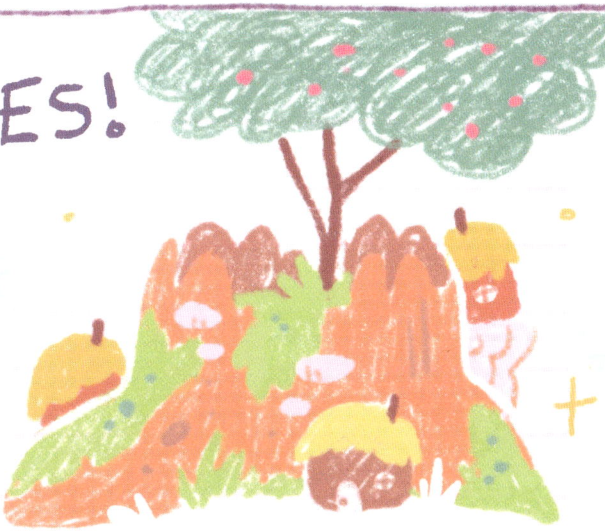

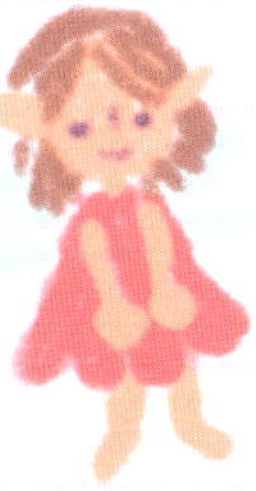

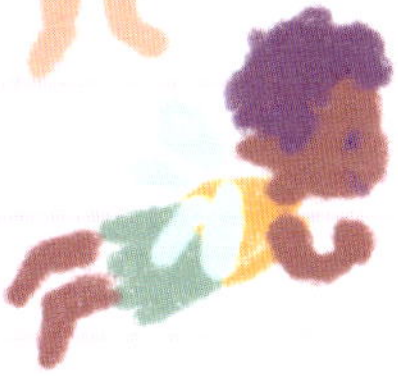

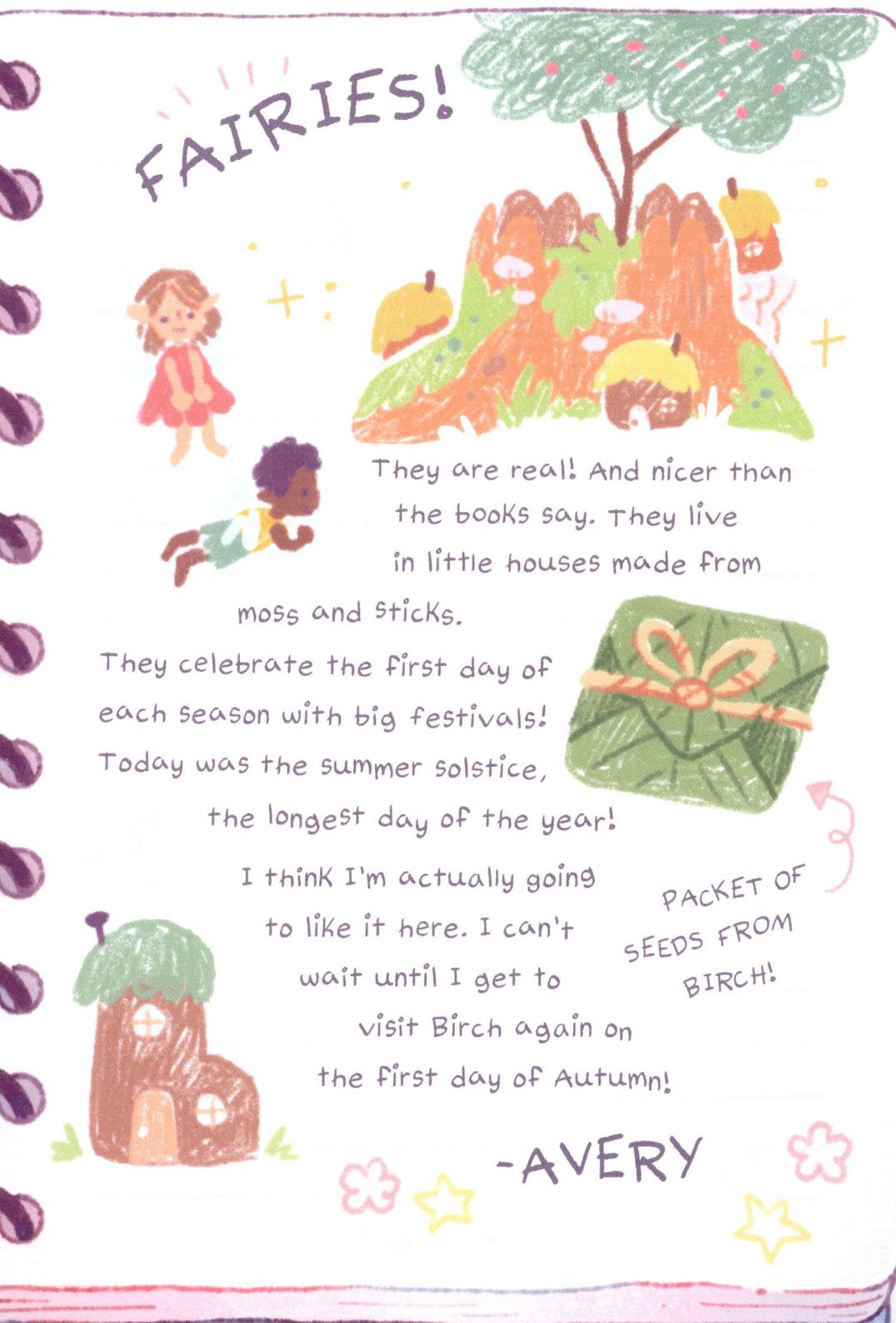

They are real! And nicer than the books say. They live in little houses made from moss and sticks.

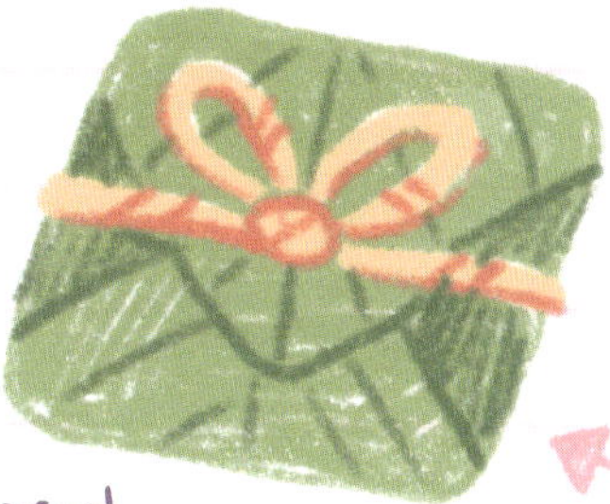

They celebrate the first day of each season with big festivals! Today was the summer solstice, the longest day of the year!

PACKET OF SEEDS FROM BIRCH!

I think I'm actually going to like it here. I can't wait until I get to visit Birch again on the first day of Autumn!

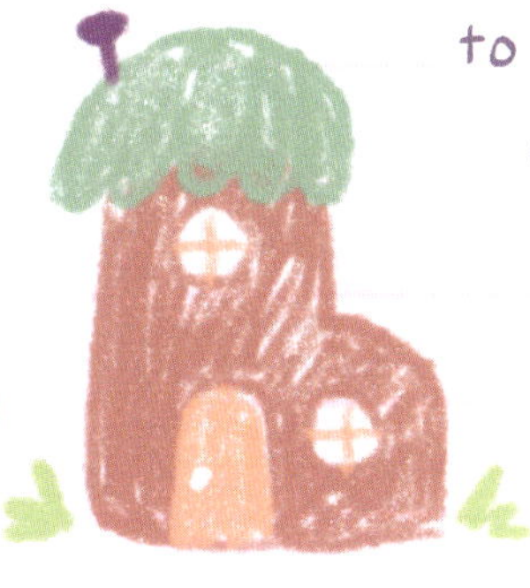

-AVERY

To Mom and Dad,
for teaching me to love magic,
plants, and playfulness, and never
once doubting my dreams.

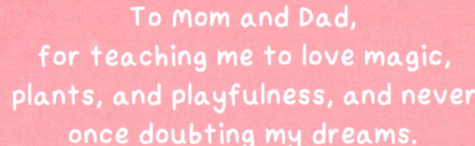

Avery and the Fairy Circle is funded in part
by the Regional Arts & Culture Council.

First edition published in 2025 by Flying Eye Books Ltd.
27 Westgate Street, London, E8 3RL.

Text and illustrations © Rowan Kingsbury 2025

Rowan Kingsbury has asserted her rights under the Copyright,
Designs and Patents Act, 1988, to be identified as the Author
and Illustrator of this Work.

All rights reserved. No part of this publication may be reproduced
or transmitted in any form or by any means, electronic or mechanical,
including photocopying, recording or by any information and storage
retrieval system, without prior written consent from the publisher.

1 3 5 7 9 10 8 6 4 2

Edited by Niamh Jones
Designed by Ivanna Khomyak and Eloise Grohs

Published in the US by Flying Eye Books Ltd.
Printed in China on FSC® certified paper.

ISBN: 978-1-83874-198-3
Library ISBN: 978-1-83874-931-6
www.flyingeyebooks.com